TRUST *Us*

LOVE ENDURES • BOOK SIX

SUSAN WARNER

TRUST *Us*

One

"An attractive man has just asked me to marry him," Pearla Isaacs explained to her empty car. "He's stable, rich, and he's sending me to a class to interview the chef for our engagement party. Any other woman would be happy, why not me?"

As the owner of a project management company, anyone would think that having everything laid out for her would be a dream come true. Pearla had been working since seven that morning when she had received the evening invite from Lance Gorman, the bachelor millionaire who owned one of the most extensive support staffing networks in New York. He had called her and asked her to marry him.

The request took Pearla by surprise, and she wasn't able to respond right away. Lance filled in the silence with the good reasons they should marry. They had complementary businesses. He'd counted their business meetings as sufficient 'dates'. They had their own money and wouldn't be offended by a prenup, but the most essential factor was they were both past that stage in their life when they believed in love. He didn't want to marry a person who wasn't a realist about life.

"I'm honored you considered me," she said in a neutral tone. What else was there to say to the man who thought it was fine to propose over the phone?

"You consistently made my shortlist when I looked at all of the factors," he said with what sounded like a hint of pride. "Do you have any objections?"

Pearla was sitting at her desk in her large corner office. The room was dark blue and grey, and her desk was a large mahogany antique. Her suit was black and loose, obscuring any hint of the woman beneath it. Did she have any objects?

"I need to think about this. It's sudden."

"No, no, no, I understand. You want to talk to your lawyers and make sure this is a good fiscal move. I get that. So what we'll do is we'll have an engagement party. If by the time the party comes, and you're not satisfied, we'll break it off. It will be an excellent social boost for us both. I'm sure your lawyers will be okay with me. If you can get your background check done in three weeks, I'll set up the engagement party.

"Lance, can we talk about this?"

"Of course, we can meet up later. I always knew you were a logical woman. I'm sure this will work for us both. I've picked the caterer for our event. I hear he's the best. I don't know his name offhand, but he's giving a class tonight. I'll have my EA get you into tonight's class. Offer him whatever, price isn't an issue. I'm leaving to seal a big deal in the morning, but when I come back, we can talk."

"Lance maybe we can—"

"I'm sorry. I have to take the other line. I'll call you later."

Three hours later, the address of the class was sent to her. Pearla looked at the address and the time and realized that by the time she got there, the class would be over. Still, someone had gone through the effort of sending the invite, and politeness was too ingrained in her to simply not go. That was her problem all the way around—she never wanted to offend anyone. In business, they all thought she was a master negotiator, but, in truth, she compromised to avoid long conflict.

Pearla knew the nickname others had given her was Ice Queen. It had more to do with her being unshakeable at meetings no matter how loud anyone else got. She used the moniker as a shield. She wasn't rude, and she never raised her voice. She was the child of a French father who thought it was undignified to yell and a Chinese mother who thought it was unbecoming a woman to argue about anything. Even after the business deal of marriage was proposed, she went back to her calendar and finished her tasks for the day.

Project management had never been her dream job—in fact, she had never liked it—but she was very good at it. After the passing of her father from a heart attack after college, she had taken her business degree and built a company that would take care of herself and her family. But she spent more time behind her desk than she did talking about projects with people.

Pearla drove her gray Honda civic with the windows down, letting in the fresh August evening air. The seasons were changing, and it was Pearla's favorite time of the year. For her, it was still light jacket weather and a great time to go for long walks. It was the temptation of autumn that was wafting in the wind.

This would have been an excellent evening for a walk.

Instead, Pearla was going to see a caterer about an engagement she hadn't agreed to. This was her life. But catering brought back memories.

Once upon a time, she had thought she was going to be a baker. Her father had been alive then. He had told her that it made sense she wanted to bake—after all, they were French.

That had been a lifetime ago.

Sighing, she brought herself back to the present. She had a plan. She'd meet with the caterer, tell Lance that it hadn't worked out, then schedule a time to cancel this engagement. What she dreaded was coming up with a reason they shouldn't get married. But unfortunately, Lance was right. It made logical sense for them to marry. Her mother would think it was the most responsible and stable thing to do. So uncharacteristic of her father. There wasn't anyone else in her life, so it wasn't like she could say she had other prospects.

She was essentially married to her job. Building a company that employed project managers to deploy across the world took time, dedication, and left nothing for a social life. She attended charities like they were birthday parties—but not dates. If it weren't a fruit, she wouldn't know what a date was. Most of the time, she didn't notice it, but lately, there had been a perfect storm of signs that she should be thinking of marriage, like her mother's morning call.

"Pearla, good morning." Her mother was always straightforward. "I know a nice man. I met his mother, and she says he's a good catch."

Pearla had attended a charity last week, where another woman had slipped her a phone number and a postcard advertisement as she spoke.

"Hello, Ms. Isaacs. I notice you always come to these events alone. I wanted you to know we are a very discreet agency for business professionals like yourself."

"Excuse me?" Pearla remembered asking in confusion.

The statuesque blonde gave a demure laugh. "Please don't be embarrassed. Our companions are professional. They pick you up at your door and leave you at your door. Try it."

The woman had patted Pearla's hand and moved on.

She wasn't lonely, exactly. She spoke to people all day and traveled extensively for her career. Pearla didn't lack mental stimulation. Most importantly, she provided for her family. Her mother and sisters didn't need her as much now, but she was always available for them.

At night her condominium was her sanctuary. It had two bedrooms and a large kitchen, which she used daily. It was true there were some nights after she had created a particularly difficult dish that she wondered what it would be like to serve two plates instead of one. Pearla could plan projects, buildings, schools and help small countries with their infrastructure, but being in a relationship had always gone wrong every time she'd attempted it.

Still, Pearla considered herself fortunate. A light on her dashboard flashed, and she heard the ding of her GPS letting her know she was a block away from her destination. She looked at the clock—the class would have ended five minutes ago. If she were lucky, she'd be able to catch them cleaning up maybe. She was going over her speech in her head.

"Oh, you're busy and don't have time. No worries,

I'll convey your regrets," she practiced. She was looking for parking when she saw a car double-parked with its hazards lights on. There were several containers on the side of the vehicle, and as she got closer, she could see the figure was faced away from her and shaking his head. She took a look at the clock. If she was going to have any chance of finding the teacher of this class, she needed to ignore this person who seemed to need help. But then her conscience prodded her. Whoever it was, they were stranded in Queens on a Thursday night. She would hate to be in that predicament, and if she were, she hoped someone would help her.

"If you look the other way and slowly drive by, you could say you didn't see them," that other evil little voice said. She let out a sigh and looked over her shoulder to make sure she wasn't causing an accident by pulling up behind the car. It was ten o'clock. In Queens, you could technically find people out at all times of the night, but on weekdays most people were indoors by ten. The possibility of another person stopping was slim.

Maybe the person knew about the class and could give her the number to contact the teacher. Getting a no on the phone would be significantly less stressful and more manageable. She pulled up behind the vehicle and then reached into her glove compartment for her mace. Helping was good, but she wasn't foolish.

As she approached the red Rav 4, she could see that the back door had been left open. Inside were several containers. Phew, no bodies, she joked to herself. She walked around the vehicle and saw a man leaning under the hood. The driver's side door was open, and she could clearly see a man as he stomped back into the driver's seat and turned the engine. Hearing the churning of an engine that sounded just like the little engine that could, made it clear what was wrong with the car.

She had jumper cables in her car, so there went the possibility that she wouldn't be able to help. It also meant the chances of her meeting the caterer had gone from slim, to none. The good news was it was just a jump. She turned back to her car and then pulled it up next to the Rav 4. She got out of her vehicle and opened her trunk, where her cables lay in a beautiful bag.

At least she hoped they were there. She had seen the floral nylon bag at the store and was immediately drawn to it. The zipper of the bag was a flower petal and the straps that closed over the top of the zipper and fastened to the handle. When she had purchased them the attendant had opened the bag and apologized for the red and black handles on the cable but assured her the color disconnect was necessary. Pearla had bought them just in case, but this would be the first time they would be used. She closed her trunk and called out to the man who was once again under his hood.

"Hello, do you need a jump?" she called out. She stopped a body length away. She wanted to help, but there was still some common sense left in her.

"Do you have cables in that cute box?" he responded. "I left mine to make room for my cases, and now my cases need the cables more than ever."

Pearla was frozen in place. That voice. It was warm like a chocolate lava cake and smooth like the melted middle. All of her concerns about stranger danger went away. Should spray him with mace and leave him the box? She couldn't grab on to a clear course of action.

The only thing that kept reverberating through her mind was, she knew that voice.

Then like a bad dream, the pieces started to fall into place. The cases outside of the car. They were food cases. Her coming to a cooking class and Lance wanting the best to cater their event. The voice that she'd never forget.

That voice belonged to Evan Carson. The four-star Michelin chef.

He was also the love of her life.

The one she had walked away from.

Two

Her father had a saying, "No matter how fast you run away from something, if you don't deal with it, you'll find yourself running right back into it." Evan Carson would qualify as something she hadn't dealt with properly. She had never expected to see him again. Not after the way they parted.

What was he doing here? Why was he here now? Why didn't he have help to move these cases? All of those questions went through her head as her eyes took him in. Looking at Evan in the evening light gave him that superhero look. The streetlights behind him accentuated his broad shoulders, tapered waist, and lean bowlegged legs. When they had been together, Pearla had told him that God gave him bow legs because there had to be at least one flawed thing on him.

His hair was short so it wouldn't interfere with his cooking. She lowered her eyes and, for a moment, remembered how his eyes were golden brown like butterscotch. She knew he had a nose with a slight bend on the bridge, the origin of which he never confessed, and a strong, sharp jawline that invited the touch.

A smile came to her lips when she remembered how she would tease him and say his lips were so red it looked like he had cherry gloss on. Then he had wanted her to kiss him to find out if his lips tasted like cherries.

Now, things were different. Pearla knew she was still shadowed in the dark, and he couldn't make out who she was. She savored watching him swagger toward her with that bowlegged strut. It would end when he saw her face, but for now, she memorized what it looked like when he didn't mind being in her presence.

Pearla wasn't one to prolong the inevitable. She could go down memory lane all she wanted, but Evan was a grown man. She drew upon her inner composure and pushed all of her feelings deep inside her heart. The reality of who they were to each other now was the only thing that counted.

"I thought when you earned those stars, they gave you a line cook for each one, and they followed you around to take care of things like this."

He stopped in place.

"No way," he said in disbelief.

"But way," she replied softly as she had so many years ago when they had been different people. Pearla took a step toward him and looked him in the eye with her practiced polite smile.

Evan was always so easy to read, and tonight was no different. Gone was the easy-going man, and in his place was a hardened man whose body stiffened, and the emotions flew across his face. She saw the hurt, longing, and then the emotional shut down happen in front of her. It was enough to make her take a half step back as if she had been physically hit.

"You can keep the box." The voice that could melt butter was now as cold and hard as an iceberg. She knew what Evan meant. He didn't want anything from her.

Pearla was made of sterner stuff. If he thought polite rejection would stop her from helping him, he had obviously forgotten her focus when she wanted to do something.

"While I understand your reticence to accept anything from a stranger, I'm afraid you are low on options and need to get yourself up and going before something tragic happens to the contents of these cases."

His gaze scanned the cases, and she knew that would be the only leverage she might have to accept her help.

"I'll call one of those line cooks."

"Evan, let's both try to act like adults. Use the cables," she said, extending her arm and the case toward him.

"I don't want to bother you. Get back in your car Pearla, and forget you saw me."

She watched him go to the hood and turn his back on her. She had winced with each rejection. Pearla thought she could take the hits, but this Evan was colder and harder than she remembered.

"Fine, you can choose to ignore me, and I'll call the curbside service for my car and then tell them I made an error. Or you can use the cables, and we can both try to move on from there," she said.

"Still bossy and thinking you can control everything, I see," he said as he straightened and walked over to her.

"I'm a project manager, remember? It's my job to

prepare for the unexpected and to make sure everyone else stays on track. Would you like to take the cables now or not?"

His brow had furrowed in frustration. He was clearly conflicted. Every now and again, his gaze would go to the box she held. He used to be so impulsive. By now, he would have already taken the box. Time had given him a little more patience, but life had hardened her will to withstand his coldness. She could wait. Patience was a tool, and she used it like a surgeon.

He took the cable box. She said nothing. Pearla turned and went to her car to pop the hood. There would be no catch-up talk during this exchange. His body language said, "Let's get this done." Knowing she had earned this and that his attitude was of her making didn't make it easier to bear.

As he attached the cables, she looked at the building they were in front of. It was called the Culinary Institute of the Soul.

"Is this your school?" She asked as he double-checked the connections.

He went to his car and turned the engine once, then twice, and then it caught. He stood up, and a smile of relief came over him. Then he looked at Pearla, and the smile died.

"The school belongs to a mentor of mine. I teach here to help her out."

"A Michelin chef would definitely do that for an institute." Pearla looked at the building and could see it wasn't in the best of condition. While the front was clean and the doorway into the building well lit, the fixtures on the side were old, and one of the sconces had a flickering light. If the cases outside were any indication, they didn't have the correct equipment either. The cases that Evan had were not refrigerator safe.

This type of gesture was typical Evan. The woman who owned this school would only have needed to help Evan once. He would come if she had a need. When they were in college together, he would always say, "You can't measure deeds people do for you one to one. It all depends on when someone helps you. They could have been the one who made your good fortune all possible. So when any of them call, be open to help."

After the cars had run for about ten minutes, Evan unhooked the cables and packed hers back up in her cable box.

She wanted to know how long he'd be here. But she could just imagine what that would sound like. She'd have to find out those details soon enough, but tonight wasn't the night. She had an executive assistant who seemed to have connections everywhere. Pearla would ask Jessica tomorrow.

"Thank you," she said. "You know, you could keep the box if you want to make sure you don't have another short."

"I'm good." He turned and went to his car. It had taken a lot for him to take the box. She didn't know why she hadn't just left it alone. Then, as she was about to enter her car, he called her name, and she peered back at him over the top of the car.

"Pearla, you shouldn't have stopped. You're a lone, attractive female. Don't let your nature make you overextend yourself. All that being said. Thank you for stopping." He said the words in a grudgingly, halting tone.

Pearla nodded in his direction and then said, "You're welcome."

She waited until she was sitting in her vehicle and watched as Evan finished packing his car. She allowed a smile to peek out. He was concerned about her helping strangers.

She was pulling into the garage of her condominium when she realized with all that was being said and done, she hadn't asked Evan anything personal.

She'd call him tomorrow and then she'd call Lance as well. That night she got dressed for bed in a large sleep shirt that said Chocoholic. She knew sleep wouldn't come easy to her. Pearla got a pot of tea and looked out of her full-length windows. Being on the sixteenth floor had its privileges. She tried to get her heart to be as calm as she was on the outside. It was crazy. It was the wrong time. But the only thing she kept coming back to was that he had called her attractive.

The years faded away when she was in his presence.

Evan Carson was back in town.

Three

Pearla Isaacs.

What kind of joke was being played on him? He comes back the hero with all the glory he promised, and when he's at his weakest, he runs into the one woman who said following your dream wasn't stable and wouldn't take care of the necessities.

As Evan finished packing the cases in the truck, he looked over his shoulder ever so often to see if she had gone. He wanted to ask her what she was doing here tonight. Really, was he so slow? It wouldn't matter why she was here. There was nothing about her that concerned him anymore.

If he were honest, it burnt him some kind of way that she was the one who happened along to save him. All the cases were in the Rav and ready to go. She was still the same. Pearla was two different women, and he didn't know which one was the real one.

Even with the warning he was giving himself, Evan couldn't overlook the fact that she was still a beautiful woman. Her hair was thick and a black so dark that it was almost blue. It had a hint of curl in it. When he would put his hands in her hair, it would curl around his wrists. Evan remembered how soft it was. Smooth as silk. But what he remembered the most were her eyes. They weren't almond-shaped but round pools of emotion. When she laughed, he could see the laughter light up her whole face. She was the perfect mix of genetics into an amazing woman.

Time had not diminished the eternal beauty she had possessed in college. That young woman who was an ingénue and hadn't found her way in the world had been a quick study. By the second year, she had her focus and bearing. Today she was a focused, mature woman whose beauty was intertwined with her confidence. If she had been attractive in school, he had to admit she was almost irresistible as a businesswoman.

So many career women complained about not being able to keep their figures. Why couldn't Pearla be one of those? Instead, she was enthralling and sleek in her movements. There was nothing ungainly about her. In fact, when she moved, there was an inherent grace that made you watch in awe.

Evan wished he hadn't noticed anything about her. He thought he had dealt with this part of his life. He thought he had reconciled himself to forgetting about having a long-term relationship, period. It was fate that he was here to help the woman who had been his anchor when he and Pearla had broken up, and then Pearla shows up. He didn't want to have to lean on Catarina to get over Pearla again.

Evan's parents used to live in an upscale apartment building and Catarina came over to cook for them. They loved each other and loved Evan because he was a product of that love. While he didn't want for anything, he was never a priority in their lives. Instead they were more than happy when Catarina and Max would watch Evan as they travelled on business and pleasure with one another. It had started with Catarina watching him in the apartment building but as time went on he would go to her house. They assured Evan as soon as he was old enough to appreciate the world they would take him. That day never came and his parents died as they had lived, together while they were travelling. They died the first year of college.

Evan mourned his parents but by then Max and Catarina were permanent emotional supports in his life. Catarina had given him a room when he she watched him at her house. After they sold his parents apartment, he moved his items into the room at Catarina's. When he and Pearla had broken up the first time, Catarina had been there to hold his heart together and convince him to go on.

Pearla was always so hard to read. Had she looked at the cases and thought, nothing has changed. Did she think he was still callous, uncaring, and irresponsible?

He knew coming back here meant facing the old thoughts people had of him. Success didn't wipe away the past. At any rate, he was home, and that meant he had to deal with the public scrutiny and lack of tact.

Catarina left earlier to prepare her spare bedroom, she said. Once he had agreed to come home and help, she wouldn't hear of him staying anyplace else. He had spent so much time in the two-family house in Queens that it would be like going home. His parents were gone, and for all intents purposes, Catarina was the only family he had left.

Evan pulled into the narrow driveway of the house. Catarina had parked on the street so he was able to get the Rav closer to the house. He stepped out of the car and had to be careful not to crush Catarina's flowers. It was her form of relaxation.

"Don't step on my babies, Evan," she said to him, peeking out of the front window.

"You are supposed to be asleep. You don't have to wait for me," he said, shaking his head, closing the door, and bringing out the cases to the front doorsteps.

Catarina opened the door and stood in her pajama pants and top. The shirt said What's Cooking? Evan should have known better. True, the lights in the house were out, but when he pulled the Rav up, the security lights turned on. If he had done what he originally said, which was take a cab to the class and have some guys clean up and come over tomorrow, he would have missed seeing her.

It was too late now. Catarina had propped up the door and was bringing in cases herself.

"I've got this," he grunted as he brought in two cases.

Catarina waved him off. "Of course you do, but the work will go faster if there are more hands."

Once he stepped inside the house, nostalgia hit him, and the overwhelming feeling of being safe and home suffused his body. It always smelled like apple pie in the air. Tonight was no different. Evan could feel the tension drain from his body, and a smile curved his lips. His moment was interrupted by a gentle nudge from Catarina.

"I see my boy needed to come home not just for me, but it seems like your soul could use some rest as well."

"I didn't know," he said in awe.

"Well, I felt bad for calling you, but when I heard your voice, I thought maybe there was a bigger plan," she said, standing in front of him and tugging his ear so he would bend. Catarina was a whopping five-foot even while Evan stood just shy of six feet. Catarina had always teased him that height didn't make him in charge. Tonight she affectionately tugged him closer to her.

"You sounded real bad, my boy. I needed you, but it sounded like you needed something too. What has been hurting your heart?"

Hurting his heart?

"Are the cases all in?" he asked, hoping to change the topic.

Catarina stepped away and shrugged.

"So there has been so much time between us, that we don't talk from our hearts anymore?"

Evan stood there and realized that time had passed, but Catarina's ability to wind him around her finger hadn't.

"I'll talk, but I want to make sure everything is in."

Catarina went to the couch and folded her hands.

"Everything is in that needs to be tonight. Close the door and talk to me."

He closed the door and sat down across from her on the loveseat. The quiet of the house settled into him. He waited to hear the light pacing of the upstairs tenant, but there was nothing.

"Your heart, my son?" Catarina prompted him.

"My heart is closed to everything but my food. Even that is getting less and less of it," he said. It didn't matter that he was a grown man in his mid-thirties, when he was with Catarina, he was back to being that gangly teen who was trying to find himself.

"Because?" she prompted softly.

"There is no passion in anything I do."

Catarina got up and sat next to Evan and grabbed his hands in hers. She brought them to her lips and kissed them.

"The heart can't be controlled. It has to be what it will be."

"What does that mean?" Evan asked, confused. Catarina was his surrogate mother, his mentor in the kitchen, and at times a wise little lady who told him things he never understood.

"It means that you needed to come home and fix your base. Remember, if the base of the cake has cracks eventually…"

"…it will fall," he finished for her.

"I'm hurt you didn't call," she said.

"I thought I could do this, that it would pass. I thought if I got more awards or just more of something that this would blow over."

Catarina patted his hands and put them on his lap before sitting back to sigh.

"Evan, you are like my son. I would hope that when you have a problem, you would call. You say you have no passion, but this woman isn't blind. I've seen you in the papers with women on your arm. Lately, I've seen a particular woman who was on your arm, and I had hopes."

"Those women don't know me or want me. They want a famous chef who can cook for their friends. The woman you saw? Well, all I can say is there isn't anything to keep me from being home with you."

Evan didn't want to talk about the woman who been there. Denise had been on his arm lately, but that was over. The life he had tried to build in California was shallow. As soon as he had run into a problem, it became apparent to him that none of it would hold up to the test of time. Everything he had invested in had gone sour. His restaurant was still there, but not even that brought him the peace that only cooking could do for him.

Catarina tapped him on the shoulder.

"You know this will not due. When you think of what was, you get a dark look that I can't stand to see on one with so much life."

"I need to rest."

Catarina stood up. Of course, you need to rest. You can sleep in your old bedroom and know I will watch over you." She reached out and smoothed her hand through his hair. "I can see you have been upset. That is the only explanation for this short hair."

Evan let Catarina's love and acceptance engulf him. He felt so raw today that he couldn't wait to get to bed. This wasn't why he had come, but he could tell he needed it.

"I fixed up your room."

"No—"

"Please, my son, you know I want only the best for you. I actually had it done last week, but today more pillows came in, so I had to put them in there."

Evan had forgotten how Catarina could make a safe haven for you so a person could block out the world. At least most of the world, because nothing was making him forget about a woman who still had the power to cause his heart to jump.

Four

He rolled over in his bed and ran into a plush dinosaur toy that made him smile. When Catarina said she had fixed it, what she really meant was she had pulled out his favorite comforter and all of the comfort toys.

The smell of pancakes wafted in the air. If he wasn't mistaken, he could smell a touch of apple sauce in those flapjacks. Evan rolled over, and the morning sun met him peeking around the edges of the drawn shades.

He had hoped a change of environment would lift the heaviness from his heart. Evan was waiting for the thrill of cooking to come back to him. He had broken up with Denise six months ago, and everyone had told him it would take longer. Evan didn't have longer than that. In fact, he found that after the first two months, he was already wallowing in depression. Every morning when he woke up, the only thing he could think about was going back to sleep.

As he was taking a shower he thought about all the things that used to bring him pleasure. He was at a point in his life when he had accomplished most of his goals.

He had money. Evan had become the chef he wanted to be, but there was still something missing in his life. He never thought the day would come, but he realized now that the thing that was missing in his life, couldn't be replaced by his love of food.

After he had gotten dressed, he made his way downstairs to the kitchen. On the table was a stack of pancakes. He looked around, expecting to see Catarina, but she was nowhere to be found. Evan picked up one of the pancakes and rolled it like a pig in a blanket. It was warm, but cool enough that his fingers didn't get burned. He figured Catarina was in the front yard tending to her garden. Instead of finding her working with her plants, he found Catarina bringing in more cases from his car.

"Why are you out here so early? And why are you moving those cases? Where is Max?" Evan asked as he went down the steps and helped her pick up the cases. At first, she didn't answer. Evan didn't think about it because she was rushing into the house.

Coming home late last night hadn't given him enough time to truly look around the neighborhood. Nothing had changed. This was the same place where he had grown up. It was before eight a.m., and while the birds were out, the streets were still empty.

Across the street, there was a church whose doors were always open. When he looked to his left and right, there were houses, but they all looked like carbon copies of one another. He remembered when he first came to Catarina's house he thought that she lived in the perfect neighborhood. Even the cars on the street were neatly parked. In his old neighborhood, nothing was uniform. There were no houses, only large apartment buildings.

When he even thought about the cars in that neighborhood, they were all jam-packed on the street.

What he really liked about this neighborhood was that there was a time when you could go out and take a deep breath of air without anyone disturbing you. It was the mornings like these when it was just him and the birds that he remembered the most. Here he could find a little bit of himself in the hustle and bustle of his mind.

Still, there was something not quite right. Evan went into the house and found Catarina about to go back out. He stepped in front of her and held his hands out.

"Whoa, whoa, what's going on here?"

"What's going on? I don't know what you're talking about? I just want to move the cases in and unpack them or replace the items if I need to, so they will be ready for the next class."

"Where is Max?"

Evan had to admit that last night he had missed the old man coming down to greet him. For as long as he could remember, it was always Catarina and Max. Max lived upstairs in his apartment, and he was retired. He was a constant figure in the house, and it seemed like something was lost now that Evan hadn't seen him yet. When he was growing up, he remembered waiting to hear the steps upstairs so he could go up to Max's place.

"You are worrying over nothing. How do you feel this morning? Was it good sleeping in your bed?"

"I feel great but—"

"I think that you have gotten up too soon. I didn't know if you would get up, but I made you some pancakes. If you ask me, I still see some shadows under your eyes, and I think you should go back to bed," Catarina said brightly.

Evan took a deep breath and gave her a smile—he thought he knew what was going on.

"Oh, I'm feeling so much better, and yes, thank you for making up my room, but I think it would be a good time for me to go and see Max, what do you think?"

Evan watched the emotions dance across Catarina's face. She wiped her hands on her pants and turned away from him.

"I think there is so much to do before you start visiting friends. Did you see my flowers this morning? I know you came in late last night, but they are so tall and colorful. I'm so happy that I planted them. I was going to plant some vegetables, but then I decided that flowers would be so much better—"

Catarina went into the kitchen and began to make him some coffee. As he watched her pull down the beans and the hand grinder, he was transported to earlier days and almost forgot about what he was initially asking.

"So, is there something you want to tell me about Max? Or maybe, more importantly, there is something you don't want to tell me about Max?"

Katarina harrumphed. She didn't even turn around to speak to Evan.

"There is nothing to say about that man. I have not seen him in a month's time," she said dismissively.

"Why, what happened?" Evan was confused, and the way Catarina was acting was completely out of her nature. Catarina loved everyone. She took care of everyone.

Catarina just shrugged her shoulders. She continued to make the coffee, and only after she had gotten everything done and the two cups were on the table did she turn to face him.

"Really, Evan, I don't know why it even matters. He was here for as long as he wanted it to be."

"Does he still live here?" Evan asked the question, but he wasn't sure he was ready for the answer. Not having Max here was like having your parents get a divorce, and no one tells you until you come home for the holidays.

"Yes, he lives here. But what he does, when he does it, and who he does it with is none of my business. In fact, what I told him was he should just stay in his place, and I will stay in mine."

"You said that?"

"What I said was that he needs his life, and I need mine." She stopped and folded her arms across her chest. "So tell me, are you like the rest of them? Everyone thinks I should be so happy to stay with Max. That he is doing me a favor by hanging around."

"I'm not saying that at all. I'm just saying it was a shock for him not to be here."

Catarina picked up her coffee cup and began to drink. Evan was lost. What could have possibly happened here? Max had always been in the picture. It was true that there were rumors that had always been around, saying that maybe one day they would get together. Catarina had always said that could never happen, but she could never explain why. It seemed like Max had known Catarina for a very long time. He had known Catarina's husband before he died.

"I accept whatever it is you want to do, Catarina. I'm just wondering, did something happen?"

"The only thing I want to say is I have made my

decision. What is or is not the issue will remain between Max and me."

With the final judgment having been made, Catarina continued to sip her coffee. Normally Evan would have let it go, but this was something more.

"If that is your final decision, of course. But I think that means we need to look at getting you some help. I can't have you picking up all of these cases by yourself and going to and fro from the school."

Katarina waved him off. "I'm fine. I have been looking for someone, but it is hard to find someone you can trust. Someone who needs to be able to come in and out of your house."

In Evan's mind, it just meant that she needed to get Max back.

"Well, while I'm here, I will be able to help out. Sometimes I may have to go and do some other assignments, so what if we ask Max to just fill in?"

"No! I do not want that man to come back here. Ask him for something? No. I told you, I'll hire somebody, and they'll come when the time is right. Until then, I will make do."

"But—"

"No, Evan. You know I try to give you anything that you ask. But this I will not do. I need you to respect my wishes here."

Evan knew when he was banging his head against the wall. As deeply as Katarina loved, she could be just as stubborn. Evan nodded in agreement. He wasn't sure what had happened, and he wasn't sure how he was going to fix it, but he was going to get to the bottom of it. Just like Catarina loved deeply and wanted the best for those around her, Evan had the same trait.

Five

"So it looks like we're going to have to do a little more work today," Evan said to Misty, his eight-year-old godchild. Misty looked back at him and had all the trust in the world in her eyes, but he could see that she was disappointed. As if on cue, her mother, Stacy, appeared. She had been working in the living room, and Evan had decided to do this lesson in the kitchen where she could see them. Misty was their only child, and he knew Stacy wanted to make sure it was a positive experience for her. With the kitchen door leading straight out to the living room, he could see Stacy looking in every so often to make sure all was well with Misty.

"What's going on guys?" Stacy asked, trying to keep her voice upbeat.

"Well, it looks like there's a little bit too much egg yolk in our mix in order to make the meringue.

"Oh, no!" Stacy said, looking at Misty, trying to gauge her reaction.

"It's not a problem, ladies—it just means that we're going to throw this batch away and start on a new batch."

Misty brightened up right away. She immediately took a step off her step stool and went to the refrigerator to get two more eggs. As Misty dug into the refrigerator, Stacy touched Evan's shoulder.

"Thank you so much for coming out. I know that you and Liam are friends, but it doesn't mean that you have to drop everything and come when he calls."

Just then, Liam came around the corner.

"Hey, hey, hey, don't put those kinds of ideas in his head. When I call, he should want to drop everything and come and help me out. Besides, I think that this is where he likes to be, no matter what. He's with two beautiful women in the kitchen." Evan smiled at Liam. Misty laughed at her dad, and Stacy blushed and said nothing. However, Stacy was not so easily diverted from the conversation. And it looked as if Stacy wasn't quite convinced that this was Evan's first choice on how to spend his free time.

"I hope there's a special woman that you'd like to be with right now, Evan. If there isn't, that's something we should probably work on right away," she said with a surety that would cause a different man some pause.

"I don't want you to take this the wrong way, Stacy, but I think you're part of the last batch of the good ones. I'm good with my work."

"Work is fine. In fact, you're so good at your work some people would even say it's an art, but at the end of the day, I think we all need someone. I mean, if you're not going to go find someone, then maybe you need to open one of those foundations or something so that you can do philanthropy."

Stacy was a school guidance counselor. She was always looking at people to make sure everyone found their passion and followed it. She also happened to be married to his best friend, Liam. Liam had just gotten over the death of his first wife. Maybe just gotten over it wasn't the right word. Penny had passed away three years ago in a tragic car accident. Liam hadn't been able to move on since. When Stacy came into his life, she changed all of that. Now, if a person looked at Liam, they would have never known that he had suffered from clinical depression and had his family worrying about leaving him alone.

Evan looked back at Stacy, and he smiled.

"I've got my work, and it takes up so much time I don't even know if I would have time to give to someone else," Evan said as he watched Misty take a step up on the step ladder and then begin to crack the eggs.

"You can always make time. Just think about it, you made time for Misty."

"Okay, okay, you're right."

"I'm not going to lecture you, Evan, but I just want to make sure that you don't find yourself in the same place that I was. That one day, you look at food, and all of a sudden it holds no appeal, and you have no passionate thoughts about what to do. A person can go ahead and do so much of the work, and when burnout occurs because of that thing they love, they are left lost and listless."

"I hear you, Stacy, and thank you for your concern."

"Well, let me stop lecturing. I can tell when my words are falling on deaf ears no matter how attractive those ears are," she said with a smile and then fanned her face before bursting into giggles.

"I agree with you about burnout, Stacy, so your

words are being heard. And I'll take all compliments at my age."

"Good, so you thinking about dating now that you're back home?" Liam laughed.

"She got you! Just when you thought she was dropping it. I tell you, you have to stay on your toes," Stacy said.

Evan groaned. "I don't know. I think I need to see what my plans are before I start dating."

"Speaking of dating, I saw an interesting article on the front page of the paper this morning," Liam said. He walked in and gave the paper to Evan. Plastered across the front page was a headline that read, "The Meeting of the dollars." Beneath it was a line that said Pearla Isaacs and Lance Carson we're going to be announcing their engagement soon.

"Is that Pearla Isaacs?" Stacy asked. "I didn't think the Ice Queen would ever get married."

Evan looked at the title in disbelief.

"I never thought she'd get married either."

"Well, I don't think it's a love match. The title couldn't be more true. Lance Carson owns the largest support staff company in New York, and Pearla Isaacs owns the best project management firm in New York called Vision Consulting. The two of them getting married is just like the two of them merging their companies. It's a smart deal but a cold one."

Stacy sniffed at the headlines.

"Well, if she's that kind of woman, then Evan doesn't need her. Evan isn't the kind of person to be moved by money. She lost her opportunity."

Evan nodded and smiled and helped Misty to get her meringue whipped right. He couldn't say anything;

he couldn't do anything beyond what was in front of him. Make sure the egg whites were separated correctly. Watch Misty whip. Every so often, Misty would look up at him, and he would remember what it looked like when he would help Pearla make a meringue.

"Well, it's a shame that she is the Ice Queen. Besides that problem with a lack of personality, it seems like she's an amazing woman. The paper says she built her project management company from the ground up."

Evan wanted to tell them she had done so much more. Evan had met Pearla when they were actually in high school. Back then, Pearla's father had still been alive. Her father had been a loud and boisterous Frenchman. Pearla's mom was the picture of calm and serenity. Back then, Pearla loved to bake. When Evan met Paula and confessed his love of cooking, he expected her to laugh at him like everyone else did.

Even in high school, Evan was built like he should have been playing sports. Instead, the only thing he wanted to play with was blenders and mixing bowls. His love of cooking had led to his fair share of run-ins with the other guys. Pearla had always been there to make sure he stayed on course. She would always tell him he had a destiny and that he needed to follow his heart.

If it had not been for her and her constant encouragement to help him find his way and learn everything he could about cooking, he would have never had the courage to go to college and earn his degree in hospitality and then go on to be a chef.

When both of them were in the kitchen, it was the only time Evan ever saw the true Pearla. It was Pearla with flour in her hair. It was Pearla laughing at how cakes came out or how they fell. That was their time—when they were both cooking.

Then one day, it all changed. When Pearla's father had a heart attack and passed away, the responsibility of paying for bills in the house, and even her schooling, fell onto Pearla's shoulders. Her mother had never worked and struggled to find minimum wage jobs to support the family. They had no family in the states, and all of their extended family was foreign to them. It had gotten to the point Pearla felt as though she had to do something to bring in some type of income. It was their second year in college, and that was the year she changed her major from Hospitality to Business Management.

Evan had been hurt, and they had argued. He remembered that argument because that had been their first and last argument.

"How could you do this Pearla? You don't like business, why would you suddenly drop your dreams," Evan had asked her.

"Because sometimes dreams have to be put aside to make sure that people can eat," she said quietly.

"You don't have to do this. There's got to be another way. Besides, you can still go ahead and work and do things while you work your way up to be a chef. You don't have to give it all up," Evan argued.

"You're right. I could go ahead and work small jobs and maybe be able to give some small amount of money to my family. Or I could choose a major where I could make better money and know that they are taking care of."

"And what about you?" Evan pressed on.

"What about me? You don't understand Evan.

I am my family. To do what is best for them is to do what is best for me."

"You're being overdramatic!" Evan spat back.

"And you're being selfish and irresponsible. I don't know what I expected, but I thought you would understand Evan."

"You thought I would understand you throwing away your dream? Then you thought wrong. If your family loved you, they wouldn't let you do this."

Yes, Evan did remember that argument in their sophomore year of college. He remembered that day, and he remembered how and why they broke up. He couldn't even say how many times he had looked back at that argument and been ashamed of himself. He had spoken the words of a hurt man/boy who didn't have a way to deal with what he thought was an earth-shattering event. She was talking about helping her family, and all Evan could hear was that she was leaving him. He was scared and lost. He struck out at the only person who had ever stayed with him. If they weren't in the same major this would be the beginning of the end. He'd go traveling around the world and she'd stay and get a 'good' job locally to support her family.

Pearla was getting married. His Pearla. The woman he had just seen last night was getting married. Now, he was more curious than ever to find out what she was doing there last night.

Six

No woman wants to see her engagement on the front page of the news before she's even agreed to it. Pearla wanted to believe that she was very even-tempered. She didn't let anything get under her skin. Pearla knew that there were some things she could change and some things she couldn't. This attitude helped her to build her business, and it also helped her to let go of things that she couldn't change. Or at least Pearla thought that was the case until Evan appeared in her life again.

It became evident to her that when it came to Evan, she hadn't let it go—she had just buried it. Now it was starting to erupt like a waking volcano. Like lava she couldn't control the feelings and it burned through her best efforts to keep it at bay. It was time to face the chef. Pearla stepped out of the elevator to find Evan cleaning one of the seven kitchen work stations.

She was on the third floor of the school, which one of the floors where meal preparation was taught. Evan was dressed in a white coat with his name stitched on it, and he had a knife in his hand that was finely chopping carrots.

He had a serene look on his face, and she could tell, no matter what else he might say, cooking was still his first love.

She didn't know what gave her away, but he stopped chopping and looked her way. For a brief moment, there was that look of welcome, and then it was gone. His features went from soft and relaxed to hard and agitated. It was probably for the best. She wasn't happy to see him, and he wasn't to see her.

Then without meaning to, she started taking in all of his tells that said he was not happy. Evan had a twitch above his right eye, and he always got a tick on the right side of his jaw. Oh yes, she remembered Evan and all of the things he did that she had missed all these years.

Just as she was within speaking range, Evan shifted and crossed his arms in front of his chest.

"I hear I should be saying congratulations to you," Evan said through a tight smile.

So that was the reason he was upset with her. If only he knew she was upset with the announcement as well. This wasn't going to make anything easier. Pearla could feel the bubbling of her emotions beneath the surface. Why was Evan mad? It wasn't like they were anything to each other. Taking an internal sigh, she calmed herself down. Pearla had her plan. She would ask him about his availability not that it would matter but she wanted to stick to the plan and then go back and tell Lance it was a no-go. In fact, she was going to tell Lance the whole engagement was a no-go.

Then it was like a slow-motion camera took over. She saw Evan clench his teeth and shake his head. Was he looking down at her? It's true she didn't become the great chef he was, but that didn't mean that she hadn't lived a good life and deserved to have an engagement party fit for a queen, even if it did turn out to be part of a great business stunt.

"I'd never expect you to say congratulations to me," Pearla said. The lava was moving, and she almost had her defenses built back up so she wouldn't be driven by insecurities and—

"Does your fiancé know that you go out late at night, putting yourself in danger?"

She stopped and looked at the man that had turned away from her. The one who had essentially asked her to choose between them and cooking, and her family. And he was talking about some other man not putting her first!

"My fiancé knows that I am not a child. I can go out at night and take care of myself. At least I come prepared with my own cables just in case."

"Well, if that's the kind of man he is… Cables or not, I wouldn't leave you on your own."

That was when the dam broke, and all Pearla could see was red.

"Funny you should talk about my fiancé. I was actually coming to offer you the opportunity to cater our engagement party?"

For a moment, Evan's face went blank.

"Cater your engagement party?"

"Yes, you know, for the fiancé who obviously doesn't know how to take care of me. He only wants the best. And you are the best Evan."

She saw him thinking it over in his head. On the one hand, she knew he would be over the moon to be given his due acknowledgment. The stick in his craw would still be that it was her.

"How much time before this engagement party?" he asked. The question threw her for a loop.

The sneer in his voice was unmistakable. She didn't know what had come over her. The lava was cooling, and she was going to stop this right now. She was just going to say that it was all a big mistake. She didn't really need his services. Her intentions were good, and her blood pressure was decreasing—and then he spoke.

"I mean, most women take care of their own engagement parties. I suppose because this is a big business deal, you're letting him drive this event as well?"

His words hit too close to the truth, and the need to defend was instinctive.

"Of course I'm doing my own engagement party, and it will be in 3 weeks."

"Three weeks isn't a lot of time for you to taste all of the different meals that I could make for you."

"Name your price Evan. We can sit down and go through the menus day by day."

Evan's hands dropped, and he leaned back against the counter. Pearla started to worry. These weren't the actions of an Evan that was upset or an Evan that was confused about what to do. She had seen this look on Evan's face before, and it was right before he thought he had come up with the perfect plan.

"Well, I can't give you my time no matter how much money you have. I've already made some obligations here at the school. However, I'm willing to compromise with you, Pearla."

"What do you mean?"

"I'll cater your engagement if you agree for the next two weeks to work here with me at the school. That way, we can cook the meals that you think you want to have at your engagement party, and I can still keep the promises that I have here."

Pearla furrowed her brow and then laughed.

"Okay, you had me there for a moment," she chuckled. "Me, cook?"

"I'm not laughing, Pearla."

She stopped laughing. "You don't have to patronize me, Evan. If you didn't want to do it, you should have just said so."

"Whoa, whoa, I'm not patronizing you, Pearla."

Pearla waved her hand, indicating the stations around them. "You actually want me to cook here? You don't even know if I can still cook."

Evan smiled. "Cooking is like riding a bike, you just have to get started again, and it will all come to you."

"You're being unreasonable. I can always come here at the end of the day, and we can go over meals then," Pearla said, trying to reason with him.

"You sound scared, Pearla. Certainly, the woman who plans everything can deal with this one little upset. We're going to be here with all of the students. It'll allow us to explore which things you really want for your engagement. I'm a Michelin chef. If I can't handle you being in the kitchen, maybe I don't deserve all those stars."

"You're making it difficult for no reason at all," she said firmly.

Once again, Evan folded his hands over his chest and gave her a big smile.

"These are the only choices I can offer if you want me to do your engagement party."

Anger didn't even begin to describe the feeling that

was clouding her vision. This was the reason she and Evan broke up. He would call it spontaneity. This man had the ability to drive her crazy. From one moment to the next, he could say a word or two, and all of her composure would be gone.

"I will not fall into this game you're playing. I'm not that hard up for a caterer. As for your compromise, the answer is categorically no."

"Ouch a caterer! And that's your final answer?" Evan asked.

"Yes, that is my final answer. Why did I even think you would be reasonable? Thank you, and have a good day Evan."

Seven

Pearla walked into her condo and slammed the door.

"I can tell I picked a great day to visit you," her younger sister, Gloria said.

Pearla saw Gloria lounging on the couch and thought Gloria would never have these problems. Gloria was young, bold, and following her dream of being a physical therapist. Her younger sister always sported a pixie cut with a dash of color in her hair, the latest clothes, and carried a carefree air of optimism around her. It was no wonder Gloria was in demand. Being around her gave a person hope. Well, it did most of the time. Pearla wasn't sure she was ready to deal with her sister now. Her mind was still on that man.

"I don't know if this is such a good time, Gloria," Pearla said, frustrated and exhausted.

Gloria unfolded herself from the couch and stood up with a big smile on her face.

"Well, from my point of view, you're looking a bit out of sorts. In fact, I'd have to say you might even be upset. I see a couple of strands of hair out of place. So, you can tell me what happened while you do your de-stress cooking. Oh yes, I've come at a good time," Gloria said. Gloria crossed the living room and threw herself into her big sister's arms.

"Come into your own home, and tell me about your day while you cook us something amazing," she murmured in a conspiratorial voice.

Pearla leaned back and looked at her sister as Gloria wiggled her brows. Some of the tension broke, and she decided to take Gloria's advice.

"My day has evolved into a complicated mess."

"Aha," Gloria said. Gloria proceeded to help Pearla take off her jacket and then get her settled in by herding her slowly but surely toward the kitchen.

"You would not believe how bossy and unreasonable men can be," Pearla exclaimed.

"Men, you say, as in more than one? Oh, I can see this is going to be interesting," Gloria said, rubbing her hands together.

"It just amazes me how they can be so intelligent in one area and then totally clueless in the other," Pearla rambled on. She deliberately chose to ignore her sister's gleeful face as she prepared to relate her tale.

"Oh yes, totally clueless. Are we doing lunch, or are we doing dessert?"

"I'm not really feeling like making anything at all, so I'm just going to whip up a quick dessert," Pearla said with a sigh.

"You do that. While you're doing that, why don't you tell me some of the juicy details of your day?" Gloria asked as she took a seat at the island in the kitchen.

Pearla took out a large pot and filled it a third of the way with water and set it on her stove. Then she took out a large stick of butter and started to chop the whole stick into even squares. The motion of cutting the butter helped to focus her mind.

"My day. If I talk about my day, I'll have to talk about that man! I just can't believe that after everything I did for him that he would be so contrary. I mean, whether he wants to admit it or no, he needed me last night, but today it was a whole different story!"

"Last night? You've definitely left some things out. I'm dying here, tell me what happened."

Pearla looked at the pot, made sure the fire wasn't on too high, and then turned to her sister.

"I'm sorry, I need to change. After being at work all day I hate wearing my work clothes in the house." With that, Pearla turned on her heel and went into her bedroom to get into more comfortable clothing.

"Please, please tell me what happened!" Gloria begged, following her into her bedroom.

"What happened was I was foolish. Last night I saw Evan, and what did I do? I went ahead and helped him."

"Whoa, Evan, as in Evan Carson, the one true love of your life, Evan?"

"I don't know I'd go that far. Right now, I'm thinking he's my one true mistake. Anyway, I saw him. I helped him. You'd think he would be a little grateful, right?"

Pearla changed into a pair of blue jeans and a floral peasant top. She reached to the side of her bed and put on her house slippers before returning to the kitchen, with Gloria on her heels.

As she walked back into the kitchen, she took a whiff of the air and nodded. "Water is ready," she murmured to herself. She went back to the pot of water, and Gloria found her way back to the chair on the island. Pearla dropped the squares of butter into the water.

"You could have dropped the stick in you know. Now the Evan thing, and the last night part..." Gloria prodded.

Pearla raised her eyebrow and shook her head. "The butter should melt evenly," she said. As she moved through the kitchen, the day's events flowed out of her, and the agitation that she felt when she walked in the door started to dissipate.

Next, Pearla opened the kitchen cabinet to pull down canisters of flour, sugar, and a small one of coarse salt. Then remembering she had nothing to scoop the contents with, she opened the drawer in front of her and pulled out measuring spoons to use. First, she scooped up some salt with the smaller spoon and emptied it into the pot. Second, she scooped up a little bit of sugar and emptied that into the pot, and finally, she added flour to the pot and began to stir it with her wooden spoon.

"Do you need any help?" Gloria asked.

Pearla waved her off and smiled. "There's nothing to eat yet, so you're expertise isn't required yet. I don't know how you stay so fit. Anyway, as I was saying, yesterday, I got this call from Lance. It was pretty late, but we've been doing a lot of business lately, so I took the call. Apparently, he had an epiphany that he and I should get engaged. It would make a great business deal, and then he says that while I think it over, we should have an engagement party. Even if we don't marry, it would be great for business," Pearla said as she stirred her pot.

Gloria made a choking noise. Pearla looked up from

the pot to see Gloria's face scrunched up as if she were in pain.

"Ewwww Lance Gorman! He makes the Terminator look cute and cuddly next to his coldness. Please tell me you told him no, thank you."

"I'm definitely going to tell him that we are not having an engagement party. But he didn't give me a chance to really speak, and then he rambled on about having already scheduled an appointment for me to go to this cooking school where a Michelin chef would be doing a class. He wanted me to get that chef to do the party."

"Ahh, that's how Evan comes in. Well, at least Mister Cold knows good talent when he sees it," Gloria piped in.

"At any rate, one thing led to another, and before long, I was standing in front of Evan, getting ready to ask him to do the catering for my engagement party, which I'm obviously going to cancel as soon as I can get in contact with Lance."

"Do you need help stirring that pot?"

"No, no, no, I'm fine, it's almost done. I only need a minute or so, then it's going to start to clump and into this kind of sticky ball, and I need to make sure I get that light film at the bottom of the pot before I put it into the mixing bowl. What you can do is reach into the refrigerator and pull out four eggs."

Gloria jumped right out of her seat and went to fetch the eggs.

"Anyway, everything was going fine before I saw him at the school. I had a plan. No matter what he said, I'd say our schedules wouldn't match. I'd go back to Lance, tell him the bad news and kill the idea of an engagement at the same time. It was a foolproof plan."

"Do you want me to drop the eggs in the bowl?" Gloria said, agreeing with her by sagely nodding her head.

"No, thank you. I have to put them in one at a time and make sure I mix each one just so. If I don't, my cream puff shells won't have a nice pocket in the middle of them for me to put the cream."

"If the plan was so good—"

"I said it was full proof not fool proof! He says to me, of course, he will go ahead and do my engagement party. If I will stay there and work with him during those two weeks so that we can go over all the recipes. Can you believe he said that?"

Gloria stopped and cleared his throat. "You mean he said he was still interested in you?"

Pearla stopped stirring. "No, he said he wanted to be a pain in my side."

"You're not really getting married or engaged. I think we could have stopped this at go if you would have just said no to Lance. However, I won't beat a dead horse. We're here, and what I hear you saying is Evan wants you to cook by his side in his kitchen. This is turning out to be an act of fate," Gloria said teasingly.

Pearla looked at her sister and then shook her head. Why couldn't Gloria see the man was out to get her? Pearla cracked an egg into the bowl and mixed it. When it was mixed in, she added another and another until all four were incorporated evenly.

"Gloria, I don't think you're looking at this clearly. We haven't seen each other in years. For him to have this kind of reaction is madness."

"That was the same thing I thought when I heard you," she said in a low voice.

"He started it!"

Gloria looked at the bowl and then looked back at her sister. "I guess I'm not really sure why it matters. I mean, we are going to cancel the engagement, right? Besides, you know what you've always told me? It doesn't matter who starts it. It matters who ends it and how."

"Well, I have to find Lance first. Then I'll tell him this won't work. I mean, he took out a newspaper ad in the paper. I can't just tell him no over the phone. I have to make sure to preserve our business relationship after all."

Then Pearla pulled out a baker's rack from the cabinet. She opened another door and pulled out a plastic piping bag that had a steel tip on it. She scooped the dough into the bag and then squished it down and twisted the end until all of it was into the very tip, and she saw a bit of dough at the end of the steel tip.

"Pearla, can I taste the dough?" Gloria asked excitedly.

"First of all, it is not dough. Do you know how long it took Father to teach me how to do this? In his words, 'This is pate choux.' It's better than dough. I can make cream puffs or éclairs with this mix. Second, no, you can't eat it raw. What you can do is get me a piece of parchment paper from the drawer behind me."

As Gloria grudgingly went to fetch the paper, Pearla put a drop of dough in each one of the four corners.

"So, you don't need the paper?" Gloria asked.

"I need the paper. I have to put the drops down so the paper won't move as you put the puff circles on the sheet."

Gloria placed the parchment paper on the baker's sheet and looked at a smug Pearla.

Gloria shook her head as she took the piping bag. "I think that was a waste of dough," she murmured.

Gloria eagerly began to squeeze the drops of pate choux onto the parchment paper. Pearla turned to fill up the dishwasher. When Pearla turned back to get the bowl, she saw the circles of pate choux with peaks on them. She was aghast and horrified.

"What are you doing Gloria? Remember, when you squeeze them onto parchment paper to go in a circle. You don't pull up because then we will have a whole bunch of pointy cream puff dough shells with burnt tips."

Gloria gave her a smirk. "Can you tell me how you have no problem saying no or correcting people when it comes to cooking, but little things like saying no to an engagement just gets by you?"

"Don't be a smarty pants. One is personal, and the other is business," she said with confidence.

"So Evan Carson is personal," Gloria said in a sing-song voice.

Pearla took the piping bag and finished the baker's sheet.

"Why don't you finish telling me about the horrors of your day while you finish putting on the rest of the cream puffs, and I will sit here and do what I do best, which is listen to you and wait for the food to be done?" Gloria said with a smile.

"You're right, I'll fix it soon enough, but I just can't believe he'd ask to be stuck in a kitchen with me for two weeks."

Pearla waited for Gloria to respond, and when she didn't, she looked up. Gloria was smiling from ear-to-ear, looking back at her.

"What are you smiling at?"

"I just can't believe that there is someone on the planet who is able to get you so riled up. And it's funny to me that the one person you said you were done with, would never talk about, and who was gone from your life, is the person who's getting you like this."

"Well, this is not the way it's supposed to be."

"I don't know. What is it that Mama says? 'It's better to have lived, than to always be so safe.'"

"Safe is what gets us where we are today. Safe is what makes sure there's food on the table."

Gloria reached out and placed her hand atop Pearla's as she was putting the last cream puffs on the sheet.

"There's a time to be safe, and then there's a time to live. All of us appreciate what you've done and sacrificed for us, but at some point, you need to do something for yourself," Gloria said with a smile. "Okay, sister moment is over, put them in the oven, I'm dying!"

Eight

Nighttime allowed the truth to come out.

Pearla loved her sister. In her heart, she knew that Gloria was right. There had to come a time when she stopped sacrificing for everyone else and thought about herself. The problem was, Gloria and her family couldn't fathom the paralyzing fear that gripped her when she thought about a relationship.

How many times could a person try to open themselves up only to be disappointed again? Pearla had been disappointed. Her family wasn't aware of the failures, but it didn't make them any less painful.

The last time she tried her hand at love was probably the worst. It was the longest relationship she'd had since Evan and the most damaging. Thomas and she were together for six months. She thought they had so much in common. He owned his own business and that was a huge relief to her. She wouldn't have to explain the long hours she put in or the emergencies that popped up that required her to leave or reschedule plans. Pearla thought it was all going so well until the day he broke up with her. That conversation was etched on her soul.

"Pearla, we need to talk," Thomas had said.

"Not now Thomas, why don't we schedule it for tomorrow and—"

"We can't Pearla—I'm leaving you tonight."

Pearla had been moving items around on her desk when the words hit her, and she turned to Thomas.

Thomas gave a bitter laugh.

"Do you know, I wasn't sure if that would even make you pause?"

"Thomas?"

"Pearla, this isn't working."

"What's wrong?"

Thomas walked over to her and held her hands in his.

"That's part of the problem, Pearla. You only want to talk and be with me when there's something wrong. I want to be with you all the time and have a partner, not a savior."

He leaned in and gave her a quick peck on her cheek before letting her hands go.

"I—I thought—"

"You thought things were fine. I could tell. I didn't disturb your life, and you got to do all the things you did before I came. You know Pearla, we're breaking up today, but when I walk out of here, I won't have to pack up anything or take down any pictures."

"That's not fair. We do things together."

Thomas sighed. "We do things that you'd do with a business associate. I think you're an amazing woman. For the last seven months, I've seen a woman who is driven in her work and loves her family. I admire you more than you know. The thing is I want a partner. To do that, you'd have to get close to me and me to you.

But for whatever the reason, I'm not the man who can do that for you."

Pearla was reeling.

"I could try—m",

"Pearla, I'll tell you something I learned from my kids. You can't force love. It comes, or it doesn't. It just didn't for us."

Those were the last words Thomas had said to her.

How did one change one's nature? She'd made a decision. She wouldn't try to go out there and find someone ever again. Maybe one day she would meet someone, and they could be friends. She couldn't imagine the level of trust it would take to bear her soul to another person. In retrospect, she realized that Thomas was right. She hadn't committed or trusted him in the relationship but the rejection left her demoralized and humiliated all the same. She wouldn't do it again. She couldn't go through the pain.

Now Evan was back. She remembered what it was like to be with Evan. Pearla remembered when she had been young and could trust. All of these years later, that girl had grown into a woman who couldn't imagine being that vulnerable again.

The idea terrified her. If she were honest, it was one of the reasons Evan terrified her. Pearla had a plan. She'd end this tomorrow and go back to her life, alone.

He knew he was wrong. Yesterday, it had seemed like such a great idea. In the light of day, Evan could admit that maybe his idea wasn't the best. If he needed any confirmation, Pearla standing at the elevator tapping her foot while waiting for him to finish teaching the class was all the answer he needed.

She might be mad but she still looked amazing. How did she manage to look sophisticated and angry while moving only one foot? She had on a dark suit that made her skin shine. Not that he was looking at her like that. It was only human to look at an attractive woman like Pearla.

It's a shame he hadn't chosen something like a roast to teach the class. At least then Pearla might have had enough time to calm down. It was the teen class on making dinner rolls. It was an easy lesson, and the kids loved watching the dough rise and double in size. He could admit he was more patient with everyone in lieu of his antics last night.

Feeling beyond guilty, Evan had confessed to Catarina that morning.

While they were having their morning coffee, he cleared his throat to get Catarina's attention.

"I wanted to say something."

In true Catarina-style she went to get some cake and cut them both a piece, even thought it was still early in the morning.

"It sounds like you have bad news. Have some sweet to help it pass your lips," she said encouragingly.

"I saw Pearla the other day."

"Ahhh," Catarina said with a small smile.

"It's not an ahhh moment. It was shocking. She's getting married."

Catarina put her coffee cup down. "Really?"

Evan let the words settle in the air.

"What am I doing? She asked me to cater her engagement party and—"

"Ohh, she's engaged, "Catarina said, nodding.

"I said that," Evan said.

"No, dear, you didn't, but no worries continue."

"I told her I'd do it if she worked at the school with me. I should have asked you. Doesn't matter though, because she said no."

"She said no and what Evan? Was it so bad for her to say no?"

Evan looked into his coffee cup. "I don't know. What I know is I sent a text telling Lance I was sorry I couldn't help him, and he called me. He said he'd work out the details with Pearla."

"Oh, no!" Catarina said sarcastically.

"Catarina—"

Catarina waved her hand to stop him. "Listen to me. This is a bad novella. You saw her, and your heart leaped again. Instead of just saying it, you've done this. Why do you kids make things so hard?"

"The problem is, she's Pearla. She has a way of making me feel unorganized, irresponsible, and childish."

"Oh yes, I can see you give her nothing to work with. I mean, only a grown man would go ahead and do something as impulsive as calling the fiancé of the woman he doesn't like so that he can spend time with her," Catarina laughed. "I hope this was not what you wanted to confess this morning? It's not me that you have to worry about."

Evan let his head drop into his hands. "I'll fix this."

"You could have fixed it when you were on the phone, why didn't you Evan? The real reason this time, and not just part of it."

"I know it sounds crazy, but when I told him she'd have to spend two weeks in the kitchen, he laughed. He said it would be more work for me because Pearla doesn't cook."

"And? Maybe she has changed?"

"No, not that much. What fiancé doesn't know that about his future bride?"

"So, are you saving her?" Catarina prodded.

"No one can save Pearla. She has to think it through. I think she needs time."

"From childish to noble intent, oh yes, I'm going to enjoy seeing this unfold," Catarina said as she picked up the cups from the table. "Well, no matter, it seems like you are a little more lively today."

"Yes, that's what panic will do to you," Evan groaned.

"Maybe, or maybe something else has been stirred in you today."

Now, as he leaned over each station trying to help the teenagers roll the dough into long cylinders, he thought she looked angry enough to take a wooden spoon and tap him on the head.

The class was over sooner than he'd like. As everyone cleaned up their stations, he turned to face the elevator where she stood. It was time to face Pearla.

Nine

Impulsive, childish, arrogant, were all the words that came to mind when she thought about Evan Carson. As his students left for the day she waited patiently. When it was just the two of them, he came to stand in front of her.

"Before you even speak, I just want to know what you promised Lance. I won't even ask how you were able to get to him. I just want to know what you promised him?"

Evan shrugged his shoulders.

"Do we really need to talk about that? It's not really important—I know I was wrong."

Pearla said nothing and waited.

"Fine, fine, if you have to know, I told him I'd teach you how to cook," he said in a low voice.

Pearla heard the words but just couldn't believe them.

"You told him you'd teach me how to cook?" she asked incredulously.

"Yes, I did because obviously, he doesn't think you can cook. How is that even possible?"

"Did you think maybe there's a reason why he doesn't know I can cook?"

"You're always happy while cooking."

"That's none of your business!" she snapped.

"What happened?" Evan asked, looking genuinely concerned. "I knew it was wrong after I had done it. Listen, it won't even be two weeks, when Lance comes back we can regroup. He said he's almost done wrapping up a business deal."

Pearla took a deep breath. Lance saying he was almost done meant he might be back in the two weeks.

"This is the same old argument, Evan. I say one thing, and then you decide what's best for me. I can't get to Lance, that's fine. You want your two weeks? You have them. Let's get started," Pearla growled as she took off her jacket and went to hang it on the coat hook. She needed to manage the possible fall out with her company and her image being engaged and then not engaged with Lance. If she could spin this then her customers would say it was a press error. Normally, she would scoff at the press but a similar situation had happened to another colleague and the company had suffered. The press had painted her unfit to run her company if she couldn't run her personal life. So this was going to work one way or another.

"Now?"

"Is that a problem? Is there some other way I could possibly accommodate you, Evan?"

Evan shook his head.

"Then give me a moment to hang up my coat, and I'll be ready to start."

Pearla straightened her back and took measured steps to get to the coat hook. She could do this. She was not going to run away just because Evan was here. She was going to act like an adult, stay here for the day and find some way to contact Lance. She had a plan. She was going to think it over and then present it to Evan. He would go along with it because it would be a solid plan as soon as she worked it out tonight.

She could do this. Evan was only a man.

Evan watched her take off her jacket and put on a white coat. He could see that her hand trembled as she buttoned up the jacket.

"Well, if you want to start now, that's fine. I have a private class coming in soon. It's going to be two students."

"I think I can assist with that."

He wanted to tell her this wasn't necessary, but too much had been said. What they needed was time away from one another, but that wasn't going to happen any time soon. Just when he was about to say something to her. The elevator opened, and the teens came in.

"Hi, you're Sam and Lisa, right?"

The girl bobbed her head enthusiastically, and the boy, who was dressed in jeans and a top—the cleanliness of which was questionable—nodded as well.

The kids came in and chose a workstation. When Pearla came to stand next to the workstation, Lisa turned and looked at her.

"Are you really going to be helping us today?" Lisa asked skeptically.

"Yes, I am," answered Pearla.

The young girl looked at Pearla and asked her the question that Evan knew would come up.

"You don't look like you should be cooking?" Lisa said, in an all-knowing teen way.

Pearla looked at the young girl with a smile on her face. "Why don't you think I should be cooking?"

"You're not dressed for it," Lisa said matter-of-factly.

"Well, there is no special way to be dressed to cook. If you plan correctly, you can cook in anything," Pearla replied.

Sam looked to Evan. "Hey, I thought you said cooking was messy?"

Evan looked at Pearla, who gave him a bright smile. Then he went to Sam and guided him to the workstation he had prepared during the first class.

"Cooking is messy when it's enjoyed," Evan said.

Pearla put her arm around the girl and showed her to the other side of the station.

"Cooking can be clean if you plan accordingly," she said, looking at Evan.

Teaching Pearla how to cook was a joke. She knew every step and every ingredient to making banana bread. She was beautiful in the kitchen. All of her moves were measured and precise. Her hair was already pulled back in a bun, and when they kids mixed the ingredients in the mixer, her cheeks glowed.

When she looked up and looked away Evan sighed. Pearla just confused him. He wanted to make sure she was okay. She made him so mad, and he inevitably did crazy things because of it. But no matter what, if they ended up in the kitchen, he felt calm. As if everything would be okay.

"There's still some bananas to mash," he said.

"Oh are we supposed to help you manually mix the bananas? Ours is done." The kids were standing with Pearla with smiles on their faces. Sam had defected to the other side, and Lisa was reveling in her girl power moment.

"I know when I'm outnumbered."

Pearla shook her head at his fake harried tone.

"There are so many of you and only one of me, but somehow I'll keep up."

It wasn't the keeping up that was a problem. The true issue was midway into the class Pearla had become the teacher.

After they had put their banana bread in the oven, Pearl looked up at him.

"This class is only forty-five minutes. Please tell me you have a banana bread already done?"

"It happens that I do. I know it's not as good as the bread you all made. And maybe you'll feel insulted eating—"

The kids were laughing at Evan, and Pearla shook her head.

"Stop stalling Evan, get the bread."

Evan had cut the bread and put some in carry-out packages just as the class ended. Lisa and Sam both said thank you, and Evan told them to come by tomorrow to get their breads. When they left, Evan looked Pearla over. She was true to her word—not one drop had hit her black pants.

When the kids had left the classroom, he turned and looked at her. Her cheeks bright a strand of hair had fallen out of her bun, and she was smiling.

"What's next?" Pearla asked.

"Would you have lunch with me, Pearla?"

Ten

Pearla had to admit she had no idea how Evan did it. One moment she was determined just to endure the day and get it over with. The next moment she was teaching the class how to make banana bread. It had been so long since she had shared her love of cooking with someone who also wanted to cook. Gloria was great, but she was obviously there for the end result and not for the joy of cooking. Then just as she was savoring her newfound experience, Evan asked her a question.

"Will I have lunch with you?" Pearla asked.

"Yes, you know it's that thing that happens after breakfast, but before dinner and usually keeps people going in between those two meals," Evan said.

"Yes, I know what lunch is. As long as it's not a bother, of course, we can have lunch. Do you have a favorite place to go?"

Evan placed his hand over his heart. "I'm hurt beyond words."

"Really, Evan?"

"There is no need to go anywhere. I'll make lunch for you, Pearla. What would you like?"

He was like a kid in a candy store. He started clearing up the counters and putting dishes in the dishwashers. When he had finished clearing up the station that the kids had used, he waited like an eager child on Christmas morning.

"I don't know what's here, Evan. Surprise me."

If it was possible, Evan's smile got wider. "Not a problem. Have a seat, and I will whip something up for you right away."

"Welcome to the restaurant of Evan. I will be your chef for the lunch menu. Sit back, I already know what you want, and I am preparing it now."

Pearla laughed at his silliness. She was excited to find out what he was going to make for her. In anticipation, Pearla watched him take out some garlic and some ginger, and put a little bit of oil in a frying pan. As the pan began to heat up, the smell of the garlic and ginger wafted through the air. Evan threw in some mushrooms and then some salt and pepper. Pearla wasn't sure where it was going, but she liked the smell of it. When he went into the nearby fridge and pulled out fresh noodles and a chicken breast, her smile faltered.

"What's wrong?" Evan asked. "I thought you liked this?"

What to say? Yes, Evan, I loved that dish when you would make it for me. Since our break up, I haven't eaten it.

"It's fine. Thank you."

"Whew! I thought I had dropped the ball again."

"Again?"

Evan laughed. "I seem to always be doing that around you, dropping the ball."

"I don't think so. I think you did really well with the kids today."

"Thanks. I find that I like teaching the kids. It reminds me why I love cooking."

Evan cut up the chicken breast, tossed in the noodles, and fifteen minutes later, he plated their lunch.

Pearla took a bite, and she couldn't help but moan with pleasure.

"Goooooooold!"

"You're a Michelin chef. You already know whatever you touch is gold."

Evan shrugged. "Sure, but it matters who says it."

With a few words, the atmosphere turned from two people at lunch to Evan and Pearla together at lunch. She tried to change the subject.

"Are you coming home to open a school?'

"No, no, Catarina needed some help, so I came."

"That's nice of you."

"I can be nice, Pearla."

"I know. I'm not saying you can't I'm just—just making conversation," she said.

"So what about you? I see you have your big company and you're one of the best project management companies in the city. Congratulations!"

"Thanks. It took a lot of hard work, but I'm happy with it," Pearla said. Even as the words left her mouth, she knew they weren't completely true.

"How do you like the noodles?"

Pearla smiled. "Well, at least they are well done, and I can tell these were handmade, so your technique is getting much better."

"Remember the first time I tried to make hand-drawn noodles, and it became that gummy mess?

Who knew that was so hard to do?" Evan wondered aloud.

Pearla had to put her fork down and laugh. "That guy who showed us his technique probably knew that making the noodles wasn't as easy as it looked."

Evan waved that off.

"Didn't he know as soon as he told me I couldn't do it I was going to sit down there and get it right?"

"Yes, that's true. I will say, though, whatever you set your mind to you usually get."

"Was that some praise? It means a lot to me that you know I finish things. I mean it. It means a lot that you think well of me."

"Evan, I've always thought the best of you. We just haven't always been going the same place at the same time."

There was that awkward moment that Pearla had no answer for. They finished eating, and then she got up to collect the plate.

"Hey—"

"No, it's only fair I clean up since you cooked. Besides, I'm just putting it in the dishwasher," Pearla said.

She picked up her plate and went to the dishwasher, which was behind Evan. Pearla thought with her back to Evan she could regroup. Pearla opened it and put in her dishes, then turned without looking, and Evan had the other dishes in his hand right behind her.

"Oops, I didn't know you'd be there," she said with a nervous laugh.

When it was done, she turned on the dishwasher and found Evan looking at her.

"What?"

"I know it'll sound corny, but, I didn't know what I was missing until now," Evan said.

Light headed. That was how Pearla felt. She had obviously slipped into another time. That could be the only answer to what was happening. Evan took a step closer to her, giving her time to move. Instead, she stood there waiting. She had tried to keep her distance all day today, but now it was as if it was just the two of them.

Pearla could feel the vibration of her heart pounding in her chest. As Evan got closer she fretted that he would hear it and then it came, the aroma of Evan, brown sugar. She didn't know how he did it but an air of brown sugar floated around him. Taking a deep breath to calm her heart and breath him in she looked into his eyes and the heat in them made her lick her lips in anticipation.

For a moment it was like going back in time. This was what it was like when they were in college together. The thrill, the anticipation and then the feeling as if they were just right for each other. Like she had been made to be with this one man, who got her.

He closed the distance and kissed her.

Impulsive, emotional, and bold, that was Evan. She couldn't do anything but experience the moment. The kiss wasn't deep or long, but it was enough to start an ember of ache inside of her. It was enough to make her realize that this is what she had been missing. She missed the passion and the warmth of Evan. His hand was under her chin giving her the choice to pull away. When he pulled back and looked at her, the moment was gone, but the realizations were hitting her hard.

She still had feelings for Evan.

"Pearla, I—"

Pearla took a finger and traced his jaw. When it reached his chin she pulled her hand back and then got up from the station.

"Listen, today was great. I want to thank you for the class with the kids. I think I need to go now."

She took off her white coat. Then she went to get her business jacket. As she dressed, she looked over her shoulder and saw Evan watching her. She thought a lot of things were going to happen today, but she hadn't counted on kissing the love of her life or having those old feelings rear their heads again.

Tonight she would find Lance and end this. Then she would have her normal life back.

Today was supposed to be the first day of her life going back to normal. After talking to Evan, she realized that she still had feelings for him. Feelings that she had put aside, and she wasn't sure she was ready to deal with them. What she was sure about was that it was time to break this fake engagement. Last night she managed to contact Lance, and they had both agreed that the engagement was a mistake.

Pearla was surprised that he agreed so readily. By the time they had gotten off of the phone, Lance had agreed to take care of everything.

This morning, Pearla's phone rang, and it was her sister Gloria on the other line.

"Have you seen the paper?"

"Gloria, I'm still in bed. Contrary to popular belief, I do sleep sometimes."

"You need to see the paper."

"Okay let me get up—"

"Nope, that's going to take too long. I'm sending you a picture of today's headlines."

Pearla didn't know what the problem was, but whatever it was, it had Gloria really upset. A few moments later, there was the ping that said a picture had come through. She took the phone and swiped up so she could see the picture. Sure enough, it was a picture of today's headline. The headline read, "The Ice Queen gets dumped!"

"No," Pearla said, looking at the title and making the picture larger so she could read the article below. The more she read, the more her heart sank. Lance Gorman, in typical Lance fashion, had spun the situation to his best advantage. At the bottom of the article was a picture of Lance and a woman on a beach. The article said that Lance decided he couldn't possibly marry Pearla. Pearla was too much of an A personality. Now that he had met Bambi, he had decided he was going to be more in tune with his emotional side. The source was cited as someone close to the situation.

"Pearla?" Gloria said on the other line.

Pearla heard her sister even though the phone wasn't on her ear. She just kept looking at the article. The only thing she could think about was how this would negatively affect her business.

She supposed she should have been thinking about him calling her the Ice Queen. None of that mattered right now. With this article, she would need to expect some fallout from some of her clients who might follow him. Lance was well liked by the industry and their shared clients. While some of her clients knew she was the best, Pearla could tell they were unhappy that she wasn't as accommodating as Lance. She didn't go to parties with her clients either. She might send them to a play but she wouldn't attend with them and their family. No they would follow Lance if he said it was better for them.

"Pearla, are you there?" Gloria asked.

"I'm here," Pearla said.

"What are you going to do?"

"I'm going to get up. I'm going to check my mail. And I'm going to find a way to do some damage control."

"Do you need me to——?"

"No, Gloria, thank you. I just need time to get this together."

Pearla hung up the phone and then laid back down. What was she going to do? How could she have been so wrong? She looked up at the ceiling for a little while longer and then took a deep breath. She could do this. She would take a shower and then make a plan.

Eleven

Evan didn't sleep well last night. The only thing he could think about was that kiss. What was he going to do? Several times he thought about calling Pearla, and each time he stopped himself. By the time the morning had come, he'd had a restless night thinking about what-ifs and second-guessing himself.

When he went downstairs to meet Catarina for breakfast, she had left him a note.

Evan, I have errands to run. Help yourself to coffee and biscuits.

Evan thought this was a great time to talk to Max. He went outside and rang the doorbell. Evan took a step back, and sure enough, Max opened up his window and leaned out to see who was at the door. When he saw it was him, a smile brighten the old man's face, and his eyes crinkled with joy. Max waved at him.

"Stay right there. I'm coming!"

Evan didn't know if Max had just been about to go out, but Max came down in less than five minutes.

"Evan, Evan, it's so good to see you!"

Max and Evan clasped hands and then pulled each other into a hug.

"I'm glad that you're still here, old man. I was a little scared that you had decided to move without telling me," Evan said. They had a long history of joking around with one another. When Evan wasn't able to find anyone else to talk to, Max had been his stable go-to guys.

Max was quiet and didn't rush to give answers. Max also didn't judge and instead would help walk you through a problem. In all ways that mattered, Max was Evan's father figure just as surely as Catarina was his mother figure.

They both took a seat on the stoop.

"So I've been reading the magazines. And you are so famous I see you in all of them, including the Spanish magazines," Max told Evan admiringly. "I told you, one day, all of that passion and drive you have would be directed toward your career. One day you wouldn't be ashamed of what you do, and you would wear it proudly."

Evan was humbled by his praise.

"So now that you are a big chef, can you come up and eat with the poor people you used to know?"

Evan laughed. "You know everyone who asks me that question can cook better than I do. And I never turn down a free meal."

Evan followed Max upstairs into his apartment. He could remember the times he had been in this apartment practicing different dishes. In fact, it had been all three of them, Max Catarina and him in this kitchen. He had played restaurant for them more than once, and they had tested all of his dishes.

Max and Evan sat down at the table, and just like old times, nothing was said. Max served him some food, and they ate. Normally, this was a relaxing moment for Evan, but today there were unanswered questions that needed to be addressed.

"So I come home, and Catarina says, you two are not talking to you. What's wrong?"

Max let out a large sigh. Then he pushed his plate away and looked Evan straight in the eye.

"Did you tell Catarina that you were coming here?"

"No," Evan responded. "She said there was something going on and—" Evan shrugged.

"This time, Evan, you need to listen to her."

"Okay. Why? I go away for a little while, and when I come back, the two people who I thought would always be here and together don't want to talk to each other. Did you know, she pulls in the cases by herself? At night!"

Max looked away from Evan. He brought his plate back and began to eat again. Evan knew this was the sign that the conversation was over.

"It can't be this way forever, can it? And if it is going to be this way, can someone tell me why?"

Max pushed away from the table and looked long and hard at Evan.

"What do you mean she is pulling in cases by herself?"

"That's why I'm home. She said she needed some help. I figured I would give some classes while she looks for a permanent answer. The school is good, but you know she always needs someone to help with the setup, and there will always be more people who want classes than what she can do."

"If she were not so picky. She would be able to find some other chefs."

"Max, why should she find another chef? You and Catarina have been cooking together forever. I know, Catarina can be hard to talk to sometimes, but something is wrong."

"A woman needs to know what she wants and what she doesn't want, yes?"

Evan heard Max and was still confused. "Can't you be the one to give in this time, Max? Whatever it is, we just need to get by it or work our way through it."

"Some things cannot be worked through," Max said firmly. "Catarina does not want me in her house. She lets me stay here, but I think I will start looking for someplace else to go."

"You can't be serious?"

"Evan things change. We all have to live with our choices."

"I understand about choices, Max. Recently, I have had to rethink a lot of the choices I thought were right. I want to make sure that you and Catarina are making the right choices and that you don't regret them later."

Max gave Evan a sad smile. "I regret nothing, Evan. What is going on, is between us two. For as long as I'm, here please feel free to come, but in this I'm going to have to ask you to leave it alone."

The morning flew by, and Evan was sure that Pearla wasn't going to come. However, as the clock struck noon and all of his students had left, he watched the elevator doors open, and Pearla stepped out.

He was going to have to tell her. There was no way he could spend two weeks with her with the way that he felt. She had on blue jeans today and a soft pink shirt. She wore a necklace with a key charm on it, and her hair was pulled back into a ponytail. Her face had that freshly scrubbed look—if he didn't know any better, he would have thought she was on her way to the movies or maybe a picnic. Her black ponytail shone as it gently swung from to and fro. He would have never thought she would be coming to see him. Without her suit, Pearla looked more and more like the woman he loved.

It took everything in him not to just run across the way and pull her into his arms. When she walked over to him and smiled, he was dazed. Her smile made him lose his thought. He quickly searched for some words to say, but she beat him to it.

"Have you seen the morning paper, Evan?" Pearla asked.

"No," Evan replied, taken back by the question.

"Good, then we need to have a conversation."

Pearla walked right past him to one of the other stations, pulled out both chairs, and sat down. Evan didn't know what was going on, so he went to the other chair and waited.

"Evan, it seems as though I have a situation and I would like you to help me."

She tossed her ponytail over her shoulder, and he watched her hair fall like silk down her back. Then he realized that she was talking. Pearla always had perfect lips. They were the kind of lips that painters wanted to paint, and artists wanted to draw. They had just a natural hint of pink to them. He thought about how those lips felt when he…and then her words started to penetrate the fog of admiration.

"You need my help?"

"Yes, Evan, I do. Something has happened."

"What's wrong?"

"If the Daily Trumpet is to be believed, the problem is that Lance decided to dump me before we were ever actually engaged," she said, huffing in frustration.

"He what?"

"A source leaked to the newspaper that Lance and I are no longer an item. Lance has now found a new woman. He will be on vacation with her as he explores his newfound love."

Evan shook his head. "Ouch! Okay, so he's using the situation to save his pride and business hide. You know someone else might take this as a sign that this just wasn't meant to be. I know you may not see that now but all things happen for a reason."

Pearla glared at him.

"Okay, Okay let me look at the article. I still think my thoughts will be the article can't be that bad."

Pearla gave him her phone and let him read the article. As he read it, he started to wince and then looked at Pearla.

"Okay, so what's your plan?"

Pearla sat up straighter and grinned.

"My plan is we are going to continue the next two weeks together. We will leak to the paper that we're doing it for our engagement, and it was never for Lance anyway."

First, he was shocked. Then there was a little tingling of something akin to excitement. Evan cocked his head to the side and looked at Pearla.

"Pearla Isaacs, are you asking me to marry you?"

Her smile turned to a frown, and she crossed her hands over her chest defensively.

"Get over yourself, Evan! This is so I can make sure that the company is okay. I have lots of people depending on me, and I need to make sure that it stays in good standing for them. There will be two socials we have to go to for the public, and then we should be just fine."

"So, what does that mean? You're not asking me to get married in two weeks?" he asked teasingly.

"No, it means that we are going to be together and be seen in public, and then all of this news will die down, and we will just go ahead and say we split ways. Besides, I will never ask a man to marry me."

Evan's thoughts were thrown up into the air. He was relieved that the engagement to Lance was over. He was even more relieved that she never wanted it anyway. Everything was about opportunity. When he graduated from college and was picked up by a chef he followed around the world it was because opportunity presented itself and he grabbed it.

Evan saw this as an opportunity. He would grab it and at the end of it he was sure that he could get Pearla to see there was an opportunity for them, if she would take it.

"Okay, Pearla, I accept your proposal."

Pearla rolled her eyes.

"So, when do you want to start?"

"The media is crafty in this town, so I think we should stay together as much as possible before we announce our split."

"Okay, then I guess that means you're coming with me," Evan said as he stood up and held out his hand.

"Going with you? You don't want to just go to my office, or I can make an office here. I mean we need to be close so the press thinks we're inseparable for a day or two. I thought it would be convenient to set that up here or at my place." Realizing that Evan wasn't really paying attention to her but putting items in his pocket she stopped talking.

"Where are you going anyway?" Pearla asked.

Evan grinned. "You know I do other things besides just stay here, right?" Evan teased.

Pearla nodded.

"Of course. Well, let's go since it's just going to be us, and I'll get working on the news release as soon as we get back. By the way, you didn't mention where we are going."

Evan smiled.

"Have you ever been to a young women's shelter?"

Twelve

An hour later, Evan had finished his class with the teenage girls. They had all twittered and taken notes. Some of the girls were a little shy, which was to be expected. However, by the end of class, even the shy ones smiled at Evan and went over the tips he had given them on quick meals.

"We want to remember that the ends of the bread are not useless. We can use them to make meatloaf and croutons if we want to dry them."

Pearla looked at the transfixed audience and then back at Evan. When they had driven to the back of the teenage halfway house, she wondered what they were doing there. Then the owner, Nancy Altair, came out and hugged Evan as if he was family.

Nancy was a rotund woman with a short afro and mocha skin. She had a commanding voice that carried and belied her five-foot-two stature. During the next couple of hours, she learned that Evan contributed to the home and that he was a frequent visitor to give tips to the women who were passing through.

"Thank you, Mr. Carson," the women said in unison.

Evan turned and told each one to come up and get a bag of starter groceries, which were covered in the lesson. While the bags were being given, out a woman came up to her.

"Are you here with Mr. Carson?" she asked. Pearla remembered her name was Twila.

"Yes, I am, Twila."

Twila seemed shocked she knew her name. "It's the first time he's brought anyone with him. Are you two together?" she asked.

"That is a loaded question, but the short answer is, yes," Pearla said.

"I hope you like us. We'd hate to lose him," Twila said in a tremulous voice as her eyes darted to Evan. "This is my second time here. The first time I left, but it was silly. When I was lost and had no money, I called him, and he came and got me. He's always dependable, and he never loses his patience. So I hope you like him."

With that, Twila went to the line to get her grocery bag. Pearla looked around, and then she looked at Evan. This wasn't the Evan she knew. This wasn't the boy who was focused and irresponsible.

Evan had agreed to help her, but she still needed to deal with these feelings. She was going to wave them off as nostalgic, but now hearing Twila, her view of him was changing. When he laughed, her gaze fell involuntarily to his lips, and she remembered their kiss.

She looked away and hoped no one could see the heat that she felt creeping up her neck. If any of the others found out about their kiss, they'd all be staring daggers at her instead of fawning over Evan now. After speaking with Twila they all probably suspected but suspecting and knowing were two different things.

As if he knew what she was thinking, he found her standing on the side and smiled.

"Well, I guess that answers that," Twila said.

Pearla jumped when she heard Twila.

Twila smiled. "I'm sorry, I didn't mean to scare you."

"I'm good."

"He likes you. I'm glad, he needs someone too."

"I don't know about all of that. We are taking it one day at a time."

"He's a good man. Because of him, I know there are good men."

Twila must have been Evan's personal cheerleader. It would be so hard to explain to Twila that she needed to keep an emotional distance from Evan while remaining physically close to him right now. That if she didn't, she'd be just as vulnerable as the women in the shelter.

She didn't like the way things were changing. She had a chance of dealing with Evan if she knew he was irresponsible and narcissistic. Evan the man, was turning out to be nothing like Evan the boy she had known before.

If she was seeing him differently, was he seeing her differently? Evan had sworn he wouldn't work with corporate types. He claimed that corporate types stole souls from people. She was now a corporate type. Certainly, the woman she had become wouldn't interest Evan. All of that made sense until she thought about that kiss.

If he wasn't interested in her, why the kiss?

That kiss lingered in her mind. When she walked by him and smelled his cologne, the heat of the memory of the kiss suffused her. When she thought about his gentleness and how he didn't push her but gave her the space to decide. She knew that kiss would stay with her.

Pearla had to get herself together. She had a plan. She just had to follow it.

Evan could admit that he had brought Pearla here to shock her.

Instead, he had been shocked by Pearla. They had already been there for several hours, and for every class he gave, she sat down with the women one-on-one on the side to help them work out a plan for whatever it is they asked her.

Evan usually had a tough time keeping everyone's interest. Pearla helped him to keep everyone calm, patient, and occupied. With Pearla's help, today's classes had allowed him to spend some one-on-one time with some of the women and also to direct them to Pearla to help them make a plan for other things that they wanted to do in their life.

Pearla had always been gifted at making plans. Today was no different. As the end of the day came, he could see that she was getting tired. This wasn't Corporate America. You couldn't work the hours and not be emotionally invested. This kind of work took more than your energy, it took your compassion. It looked like Pearla had more than enough to give.

Evan marveled that she hadn't complained once today. Although he had seen her slip out to get some water and then come right back in to answer some more questions as long as the young women came by.

He thought about telling her that they should leave early. But they had already seen the schedule for the day posted on the wall. The posting stopped him from making an excuse that there weren't any more classes scheduled. If Pearla thought the only reason he was leaving was for her, she would dig in her heels and stay anyway.

His Pearla was determined, stubborn, loyal, and fierce. He felt ashamed now that he thought she was so shallow that she wouldn't be able to work in the shelter. Truthfully, he expected her to see the sight and then offer some money to get out. Much to his surprise what had really happened was a confirmation that the woman he knew was still within her and that he was truly and deeply in love with Pearla.

All of the classes were done, and the only thing he could think about was getting to Pearla and taking her home. Just then Nancy came up to him.

"Thank you, Evan," Nancy said as she tapped him on the shoulder. "You did real good today."

Evan nodded at Nancy and then looked over to make sure that Pearla was okay. She was still talking to a young woman, but he could tell that she was hanging on by a thread. It was the slight bend in her back. It was the way that she tucked her hair behind her ear. Regardless of how she was feeling, her voice never changed. She was smooth and calm the whole way.

Nancy snickered. "Evan, you've got it real bad."

"You don't even know the half of it."

"Well, I can tell you she's a hard worker. She didn't look too sure when she walked in the door. After she heard you give the first class, I didn't have to tell her a thing. She went through the crowd and found the women who needed her help. You've done real good with this one."

Evan nodded in agreement.

"I'll see you next week?" Nancy asked.

"Yes, I'll be here," Evan answered.

As Nancy walked away, she told him, "You two make a good team."

Evan watched Nancy disappear down the hall. The funny thing was, Evan agreed. He and Pearla did make a good team. Now the only thing he had to do was convince Pearla.

Thirteen

Pearla would never admit it, but she was happy that Evan was taking her home. She rested her head back against the seat and looked in the side mirror. They had gone for a couple of blocks when Pearla noticed a car that seemed to be following them.

"Evan, can you pull over to the side, please?" she asked.

"Excuse me?" he asked, confused.

"I want you to pull over to the side as if you're going to double park for a moment, please." She could tell that he didn't understand why she would want to do such a thing, but he did it anyway. And sure enough, when they pulled over the small, sporty car behind them pulled over as well.

"I knew this was going to happen. I guess I just didn't expect it so soon." Pearla said with a huge sigh.

"Can you tell me what's going on?" haven't asked.

"Look behind us. There is a small black car with the license plate starting A-L-T. It's been following us for the last two blocks. I don't think they were with us when we went to the shelter, but it's been with us for sure for the last two blocks."

"Who are they?"

Pearla gave a wan smile.

"Welcome to my world, Evan. That very diligent person in that little vehicle is a member of the press. I knew that they would be following us at some point, but the story just came out today, and I thought I would have a little more time."

"What do you want to do? Can we call the cops?"

"No, it doesn't work that way. If you call the cops, then they'll think you have something to hide and stalk you twice as much. Let's just go to my house, and then we'll make a plan."

Evan shook his head. "No wonder you're so good at making plans. You have to make them all the time."

Pearla laughed. "I suppose I do."

He followed her into her condo. It was dark for a moment and then she turned on the lights. She heard Evan say, "Nice," and she smiled to herself. Not that it mattered what he thought, but she was happy he liked her condo.

"Come in and make yourself at home. We may have to wait a bit before you leave."

Evan shook his head. "Thank you for thinking about me, but I'm good. I'm used to the long hours. I'll be fine driving back."

"I would like to say my motives were altruistic, but they're not. You can't leave now, because the press is outside. It's so late, and you're supposedly my fiancé. You wouldn't leave right away. In fact, you may have to stay all night."

Pearla watched Evan turn three shades of red. "Pearla, I think we should talk about this."

"I'll bring you covers for the couch. Don't worry, you're safe," she said with a laugh.

Evan nodded. "I need my charger and notes from the car."

Pearla nodded. "Take the keys."

Pearla heard the door close, and she went to get into her pajamas. Today had been hard, but she had enjoyed helping each and every one of those young women. Pearla had doubts before she even followed Evan. Now that she had spent time with him and seen him be so compassionate and understanding it was harder than ever to hold on to her negative preconceptions.

What did she think about Evan now? Now when she thought about him he was Evan the crusader in the shelter. Evan was getting under her skin and becoming the man she dreamt about instead of the man she wanted to forget. Now amidst all of her confused emotions she was going to have Evan as her guest.

If his actions today were any indication, he was going to be super attentive to her needs. He showed his attentiveness to her when she got in his car and he brought her home. She had been exhausted and Evan had brought a bottle of water to give to her.

Her reflections on Evan's actions were interrupted when she heard the bathroom door open and Evan stepped out.

"Pearla?"

"I'm here. I didn't leave." She had changed into her dark blue pajamas. "I'm sorry. I don't have any spare clothes for you, Evan."

"I'm used to sleeping in my clothes, but thanks for trying. Are you hungry? Is there something I can whip up for you? That kitchen looks amazing."

She could hear the eagerness in his tone.

"Go ahead, look around, but if you keep this up, I'm going to think you only want to hang around me when I'm in a kitchen."

He looked up and held her gaze.

"It's not the kitchen—it's definitely the woman," he murmured.

And in an instant, she was no longer tired. He was teasing, but her response to Evan was very serious. It made her breath catch, and she broke their locked gaze. It was a fluttering in her stomach, and then slow heat wound its way through her body.

"PB&J."

Evan laughed out loud. "You want me to make you PB&J in this gorgeous kitchen?"

"If you want to make something for me, that's what I want. Surely a chef of your stature can make the staple PB& J," she teased.

Evan held his hands up and bowed his head.

"Of course I can make the staple. It's just today you stepped up and helped me out at the shelter. I thought you might need something a little more substantial to eat. I can be concerned as your friend, can't I?"

Pearla had her answer ready to go. She was going to tell him he was bossy, and he never learned. Then she heard him say they could be friends, and all of those petty answers fell away.

Friends with Evan? In a crazy world where everyone wanted something from her, she could now say that Evan didn't want or need anything from her. In her world she was always worried that she would disappoint people. Friends with Evan. She had already looked at all of the "old crimes" he had committed against her. None of those things fit the man he was today. She had been anything but friendly to him, but when she asked him for help, he was there and willing. She knew he was there for her and not for what she did or didn't do for him.

Maybe it was the day. Maybe it was the exhaustion. Maybe it was just to get a PB&J, but she nodded. Evan's face lit up. There was a moment of panic where she wanted to take it back, but she breathed through it.

"Okay, friend, I'm going to put together a PB&J you've never experienced."

She sat at the island in the kitchen and took deep breaths. She had cracked the door to let him in. She hoped she didn't regret it.

Now Evan understood Max's old saying that you could never understand a woman—you just have to accept her.

Where was the sense in having a talented chef in your home and then asking him to make you a PB&J sandwich? Like the rest of this day, he was thrown into a tailspin by Pearla. One moment it seemed like she was holding the past against him. The next moment, she was like the girl next door that he was trying to get to know better.

He wasn't sure if she was trying to keep him confused and on his toes or if she was just putting him through the wringer for the past. It didn't matter. He would still stay here no matter what to see how it all turned out. Now that he knew what his feelings were for her, the only question left was how to find a way to turn this whole situation around so both of them could be happy.

"Where are my ingredients?"

"Just open the fridge, and on the third level you'll see a container. It has everything you need in it."

"A container?"

She looked at him with a raised eyebrow and crossed her arms over her chest.

"I happen to like PB&J."

Evan turned away to hide his smile. His life was becoming one huge roller coaster. A couple of weeks ago, he was thinking about what was left for him to do. He was wondering if there was anything else he could feel passionate about besides cooking. Now, he was in the kitchen of his one true love getting ready to make her a PB&J sandwich of all things. He reached in and pulled out the container. When he turned back to the island, Pearla was laying out place settings.

When he hesitated, she spoke.

"Just because we're having an informal meal doesn't mean we shouldn't have the proper settings."

"It's your house, I'm just the chef here."

"I know you probably think that I have a problem with perfectionism or that I think everything has to be my way. But the truth is I'm just a creature of habit."

"I get it. Maybe it's because you've been doing everything on your own."

"Maybe."

Evan whipped up the sandwiches, cut them into fours, stacked them so that they all made a teepee shape, and then put them in front of them at their respective place settings.

She looked at the sandwiches that he had made,

amusement sparkling in her eyes, but she said nothing.

"Sandwiches are served," Evan said in his most regal voice.

He took a bite out of his sandwich, and a moan of pleasure came unbidden from his lips. He could see her smiling at him.

"Okay, what is in the peanut butter and jelly?"

Like a kid with a secret, her smile got wider.

"The jelly is organic and specially made for me by a customer I helped. The peanut butter is just regular off-the-shelf organic, but it's the bread that's amazing. It's a honey whole wheat. I keep it all in a container so that my sister Gloria knows better than to eat it."

"Okay, you got me with this one."

They were halfway through their sandwiches when Pearla spoke.

"Okay so it turns out that you are not only a famous chef, but you're also working at the shelter. How long have you been doing the shelter work?"

Evan swallowed the last bite of his sandwich.

"I started the shelter work a while ago. It wasn't really my idea, truth be told. I went with a friend one day, and afterward, I was so moved by what I could accomplish there and how much I could empower them with skills I took for granted, that I went back. I know you didn't have a lot of time with her, but you'd find that Nancy is amazing as well. I can't make it there all the time, so I try to enlist some of the other people I know in the trade to help out. I manage to get some of the other chefs to help out in different states as well."

"So I can see you haven't just been globetrotting the world. The shelter work—is this what you do to relax after you've finished eating in all the finest restaurants, going to the best hotels, and attending the big conferences?"

"I'll admit having a reputation as a chef does give me a lot of perks. It could easily make a person feel entitled to those things."

"But not you? And what about the social life you're supposed to have? Being one of the better chefs, young, and with a great reputation, all of that put together seems like you should have someone special in your life."

"Oh, you mean like a girlfriend or wife or someone on the horizon, at least?"

Pearla nodded. "I can't see anyone not wanting to be your wife. You don't have any kids. Your looks say that you've got great genes to pass on. There's nothing wrong with your kissing technique. A lot of people would say, with those attributes—plus you have your own money—you're the full package. Now, I'm going to ask the question that everyone's going to want to know. What's wrong with you?"

Evan laughed. Was this the time to admit the problem was her? How did you tell the woman that you love that you've never married because you've always been waiting for her?

"You get straight to the point, don't you Pearla?"

"It's a gift. I'm a project manager. I need to be able to assess the situation and find out what my risks are pretty quick. Consider this the risk and assessment phase. Now give it up, Evan, what's wrong?"

"I'm particular."

"With all of those good qualities, I could probably find a couple of women who would go ahead and remake themselves to fit your list. Certainly, you've gotten close?"

"Close is a relative term. But, I think I've been close once."

"And?"

"We woke up one day and realized we didn't want what the other one wanted. You know there's an old saying that says correlation doesn't mean causation. I think that Denise and I were doing the same things, but we didn't want to end up in the same place. I always wanted to come back here. I wanted to come home to give back to my community. She couldn't imagine not traveling the world and giving to everyone. I was glad that we found out our differences, but it was still a hurtful moment."

"You fixed it before it was permanent. Certainly, that gives you some kind of closure about the whole thing."

He listened to Pearla talk about the closure of knowing that he didn't make a mistake and having to live with it. He didn't say anything about the guilt he felt for not knowing himself or being able to articulate well enough to Denise what he wanted in the beginning. While he was glad they didn't marry, because neither one of them would have been happy, he had questioned his own vision and if he was fit for a relationship. At the end of the day, he didn't think he could be fair to any woman because he already had the ideal woman in his head, and she was sitting in front of him.

"So it's time for you to fess up Pearla. It's time for you to talk about your near misses."

"Reach in the refrigerator and give me a cola. If you want me to talk about this, I'm going to need some comfort food."

"It's a drink, Pearla."

"Cola is the easiest way to digest sugar. It's my comfort food. Now hand it over if you want to hear the story."

He passed her the small can and waited until she had taken her first sip. "So, any close ones?"

"So close, I picked a dress," she said in a low voice.

"That's close."

"I was engaged to a lovely man, actually. He owned his own company. I owned my own company. Somehow, I thought both of us being business owners with the same amount of gross income equaled commonality."

"What happened?"

Pearla took another drink of cola, and he watched her blink a couple of times.

"Our story was like yours. Thomas and I were working toward the same goals and realized we weren't going to end up in the same place. It wasn't even close. It turned that he wanted someone who understood that business had a place, and life had a place, and I wasn't that one."

"So the two of you broke up because you're a workaholic?"

"Partially." She stood up and began to stack the plates on one another. When that was done, she gathered the placemats as well.

"Okay, so how did you all break up?"

"I didn't realize you'd want to hear the train wreck frame by frame."

Evan didn't want to hear every detail, but he felt like he needed to if he was going to be able to have a chance with Pearla.

"He came in one day and told me he had found

someone else. He couldn't be with a woman who wouldn't give him the same amount of time that I gave business. I decided that I couldn't be with a man who thought I was cold and unfeeling. I mean, he didn't really say those words, but by the time he finished explaining, it was apparent he felt as though I had more passion for running my company than I did for our relationship. They don't call me Ice Queen for nothing."

Where did she find these men? How could anyone who knew Pearla think that she was an ice queen? He could see that the words had embedded themselves in her heart, and she was hurting. Even as she repeated the words he knew, they dug into her and buried deep into her psyche.

"Since we're baring our souls, I guess I have to ask, did you give him the time and show the care and compassion that I saw you give today at the shelter? I can't imagine any man who had seen how dedicated and passionate you were today would ever say you were cold."

She paused and gave him a long look.

"I don't know. I gave him what I thought was the safest thing at the time. Maybe I waited too long. I don't know. But he didn't see any of the inklings of passion that you see in me."

"Then you're better off without him. Being in a relationship isn't about meeting someone and knowing them, and you're one and done. It's about meeting a person and then being able to learn and grow with that person. So, if he can't see how passionate you are now, he's not going to be any good at seeing the changes in you later. So to him, we say, 'Off with his head!'"

He watched Pearla laugh at his antics and saw the tension drain from her shoulders.

"So you've gone from Chef to Chief. Oh, what a difference the letter i makes. Thank you."

She was smiling and happy, but Evan needed to know something else. Something that would change the way he was going to have to approach this.

"So is your heart mourning Thomas?"

"Ah, the million-dollar question. I don't think I'm mourning him. I think I'm mourning not being in a relationship. It's sad to say, but I think I'm more distraught that I picked the wrong one again and got so close to being married."

"Are you ready for a new man in your life?" Pearla's head popped up, and her eyes grew twice as large.

"And you say I'm the direct one?"

Evan shrugged.

"I don't think I'm any good at those kinds of things. I mean, I don't think I'm any good at picking or the relationship part."

He heard her, but she hadn't seen herself through his eyes. Pearla was made to be in a relationship where she could give and get. Her compassion and empathy made her twice as attractive as any amount of money or superficial beauty could do.

"I'm curious. What would a man have to do to make you want to try again?"

Fourteen

Oh, my goodness. Did he really just ask me that?

Nothing moved in the room. She wasn't even sure she was still breathing. Pearla's throat had gone dry. She looked into Evan's eyes, and in them she found nothing but sincerity and hope. This was what she had been waiting for. She wasn't sure what her plan was. She wasn't sure she could even make a plan for this. For once, the plan didn't matter.

She could do this. They were both sitting and the countertop between them gave her the strength to be bold as they both moved towards each other. Pearla reached out until the tips of her fingers were on the side of Evan's jaw. She traced his jaw from his ear all the way down to his chin and then worked her way up until her fingers had lightly traced his lips. Her fingers trembled, and she couldn't hide her uncertainty. Then she leaned forward and touched her mouth to his.

She could taste the jelly on his lips. The next moment she took her hands and braced them against his shoulders as she leaned into the gentle kiss. Beneath her hand, she could feel the tensing and bunching of his muscles as he contained himself to give her the time to adjust. It was the control he had, and consideration for her that emboldened her to indulge in the kiss.

She pulled back and looked him in the eye. She could feel the steady beat of his heart as his chest vibrated beneath her hands. After what seemed like an eternity, she gave in to the urge to kiss him again.

This time when she leaned in, she felt his hand come up gently behind her head and weaved his fingers through her hair. He angled his head to deepen the kiss, simultaneously pulling her closer into his embrace. Pearla's heartbeat quickened, and her hands flexed on his shoulders as the intensity of the moment washed over her. Just when she was sure that she was going to be swamped by the heat of the moment, Evan pulled back.

The only sound in the room was their rapid breathing.

"You have so much to give Pearla," Evan murmured. "There's nothing wrong with your ability to choose. People aren't as consistent as plans. Have faith. There's someone right here who wants to love you."

His words seeped into her soul. She quickly tried to blink away the tears that threatened to fall. There were no words. She didn't know how he had known what to say. Pearla had spent a lifetime hiding her fragility, and Evan saw right into it. He made her want to bask in the possibility that he was right.

"What are you doing to me, Evan?" she murmured.

His hand trailed from her hair down her neck until he cupped the side of her cheek.

"If rumor has it correct, I'm here to make you an amazing peanut butter and jelly sandwich and then share an unforgettable kiss with the most amazing woman that I know."

She gave him another look, and still, there was a shred of disbelief that lingered in her.

"Well, if the papers are to be believed, you've known a lot of women. I don't want you to feel like you're being forced to say something in the moment."

"Oh Pearla, if only you knew how simple I was. There's no need for me to fake this, because it's true. After that kiss, how could you even doubt how amazing you are? Do you think if kissing you wasn't amazing that my heart would be pounding the way it is? Or that I would have to pace my words to make sure I could catch my breath."

It seemed so easy for him. Pearla had come close to marrying someone, and she hadn't even known that she was alone in the relationship the whole time. She hated this insecurity she felt. She had no plan, no assurances about what she was doing. Would she even be able to survive this if it went wrong with Evan? To kiss Evan was to taste ambrosia, and to be in his arms was to know a safety that she had never known before. She hadn't even agreed to anything, and if he left now, she knew she'd be hurt. She knew now what could be between her and a man, and there would be a longing for it that she had only gotten a taste of. How could she have let this happen? What was she doing?

"Pearla, stop running in circles. You're thinking so much I'm getting a headache."

"I don't think we are thinking the same things at all."

"You know me, Pearla. When we talk, we hold nothing back. You won't have to wonder if one day I'll walk in and say we're done. Don't run from us."

Pearla took a step back and then took a deep breath. Why did he have to be so good now?

"I told you I'm not really good at this whole relationship thing," she said defensively.

"Right now, it doesn't matter if you think you're good at it or not. Pearla, we are in a relationship."

"Yes, we're friends. We don't have to be more than that!"

"Is that what you want? Will you push away the possibility of us having something that very few people find because you're scared?"

She wasn't going to do this. He didn't understand. Evan could never understand what it was like to be helpless, thinking that you had given everything you could in a relationship, only to find it meant nothing. With every failure, it was another mark against her. Everyone saw the men in her life as being great, personable, and outgoing, so the problem always wound up being her. At that moment, she couldn't hear anything he said. She just felt the frustration and anger sweep over her at how it was always her fault.

Her anger over not being good enough bubbled up. Anger over not being able to see far enough reared its head. Right now, though, she was angry that Evan had brought all of this up and messed up her plans and thrown her world into chaos. She had asked him to do one simple thing. She hadn't asked him to worm his way into her heart. She hadn't asked him to give her a taste of what it could be if someone could love her for her.

Pearla turned away and took care of the placemats.

"Let me help you Pearla," Evan said as he went to put the dishes back into the cabinets.

She stepped in front of him and took the plates out of his hand. She turned her back to put them up and lost her footing. All the dishes fell to the ground. The china was sturdy and broke into large pieces on the floor. Pearla was transfixed by the moment. She saw the broken glass on the ground, and all she could think about was herself. She was just like the glass on the floor, broken.

They had fallen into mostly large pieces, but there were also some small pieces that would never be recovered. She didn't know she was crying until the first tear hit her hand. Then she looked up, lost and confused at Evan.

He didn't say anything. Instead, he stepped over the glass and then guided her out of the kitchen. They made it to the couch, and he held her in his arms as the tears fell.

"Pearla, I'm sorry."

She let her lids fall and the tears with them. In his arms, she felt safe. Safe enough to cry about all that she wasn't. She didn't have to worry that he'd be disappointed with her and that he would think less of her. With Evan, she knew she could just be. She didn't know how long she cried. She couldn't even remember when she stopped. She could only remember that she was safe, and for once, she could just be.

<h1 style="text-align:center">Fifteen</h1>

Pearla knew three things: she was on her sofa, she was alone, and the smell of cinnamon was in the air. That meant Gloria was in the house. She opened her eyes but hadn't moved the rest of her body. She didn't need to, to see Gloria sprawled across the love seat.

Where was Evan? It didn't seem like he was here. It was probably for the best because as it stood, she wasn't sure what she could say to him. Who was she kidding? She wasn't sure she could even face him again.

Having him give her teases of what could be were one thing, but having him see her break down, that was something else. All of her planning and control had been tossed away in a moment. This is what she got when she did things without a plan. Pearla closed her eyes and let out a slow breath. This wasn't Evan's fault. The tears that had happened were a long time coming.

The room was dark, and rays of early morning light peeked through her blinds. She heard Gloria's soft snoring, and all of those sounds brought a calm to her that she hadn't felt in a long time.

When she did try to move, she felt the ache that came from being in one position too long. If she wasn't mistaken, she might have a cramp in her neck from laying on the pillow at such an odd anger.

"Don't move too fast. If you do, the pain will just shoot up into your head, and you'll have a migraine," Gloria said. "Try to move slowly.'

"I didn't mean to wake you."

Gloria opened her eyes and peeked at Pearla.

"It's almost time to get up and eat. I came early this morning and found an attractive man holding you in his arms. I thought for once I had finally caught you taking care of you. The gorgeous one was very chivalrous and left."

Pearla closed her eyes again and hoped the heat she felt on her cheeks wasn't really there. When she opened her eyes, Gloria was looking at her with a smirk on her face. She knew what was coming—the questions she didn't want to answer.

Slowly, she sat up and stared at Gloria.

"I need time to prepare for the inquisition," she said.

Gloria clapped her hands. "I'll be gentle with you. We'll start with simple things. You spent the day with him, and I assume he's part of the new plan you came up with. Is he as shallow and irresponsible as you thought he would be?"

"No, I was wrong. He's grown up and changed."

"Really? And what do you think about the new Evan?"

Well, that was the problem now, wasn't it? The question was how she felt about the new Evan. The answer was that she was engaged to this new Evan.

"He's got all of the good-looking attributes, and he's a good person on the inside as well."

Gloria sank back into the sofa.

"Whew! You had me worried there. For a minute, I thought you were about to do some sort of self-sacrificial self-sabotage move on me."

Pearla frowned. "I have no idea what you're talking about."

Gloria waved her on.

"No worries, we can talk about that later. I need to know how you got him to the condo."

Pearla gave Gloria a lopsided grin. "I'm afraid I'm going to have to disappoint you. The new plan I made was to be engaged to Evan. We were out together for the day. After we left the last place, I noticed the press following. I had to bring him home to distill any rumors."

Gloria nodded. "I'm going to have to use that one."

"Oh, stop it, you. He came in, and we ate."

"Good, good I can see this going places."

"Stop thinking Gloria."

"Listen, I have to help you. Most things happen on the fly. You need some spontaneity in your life."

"And you think Evan is that?" Pearla asked.

"What I think is you have puffy eyes. Since you aren't cursing his name, it means that for some reason, you were crying last night, but it wasn't his fault. You both love cooking, and he's helping you with this hare-brained plan. I'm seeing nothing but positives for this man."

"Well, you think all you want. I'm going to take a shower, and then I'll cook."

Gloria laid back on the loveseat and sighed. "I must be close, because you're using my weaknesses against me."

Pearla left to take a shower. It took moments to get the shower ready. When she stepped in, the feel of the water beating down on her skin was as welcome as a massage. The water relaxed her and gave her time to think. Gloria's question rolled around in her head. What did she think of Evan?

First, he was a great kisser. More importantly, he didn't push himself on her. He let her set the pace. It said volumes for him as a man. She knew he helped her to look at her strengths and not her failings. When she was with him, she knew it meant change. How often had she told her company that change was good? Now that she had to change, it was a different story.

She wanted to be a whole woman for Evan. Evan didn't seem to mind the fractured state she was in, but she did. She knew Evan wasn't Thomas, but the fear was still there that one day history would repeat.

Pearla let the water wash over her face and ease the tense muscles in her back. Maybe Gloria was right. She was self-correcting in a non-healthy way. She was probably worrying about nothing. After last night and him not being here in the morning. Evan was probably thanking his lucky stars that he saw Pearla like she was.

If he was smart, he'd realize Pearla Isaacs was a whole new ball of wax.

Sixteen

Two days had passed, and Pearla had gotten no response from Evan. She had left a message for him on his phone, and she had sent him the invite to the charity she had to attend. The charity event had been planned long before, but this would have been a good time to reinforce their engagement.

In some ways, her original opinion of Evan was confirmed when he didn't answer. All of her doubts seemed to point and say, I told you so. She needed to have this moment to fight the nights when she let her imagination take root, and she dreamed of a time when she would be able to walk hand in hand with him. Dreams were for the land of make-believe, and these actions just showed her that's where they needed to stay.

Every year Pearla attended the charity for new businesswomen. She wasn't required to speak, just show her face, give a check, and then quietly leave. She had dressed in her traditional black pantsuit. Her hair was pulled back in a bun, and the room was abuzz around her. She held her head up and went to the bar to get seltzer water. After the bartender had poured her soda and she left a tip, a masculine arm reached around her for a can of cola. She didn't know who would be so rude, but she was sure it was some guy's version of getting her attention. There were always a few at these gatherings.

"I'll move aside," she said, pulling herself up to her full height and preparing to turn to give the man a stern look.

Before she could turn, she felt the man step closer to her, and the encroachment in her space gave her purpose and speed. She turned and threw her drink on him. She looked up and saw him.

Not a rude stranger at all.

It was Evan.

He had come! She had to contain herself from giving more than a sedate smile. Then she looked at the dripping front of his suit jacket and murmured, "Oh, no."

"This seems to be a pattern. You having accidents around me. I have to ask, are you clumsy, or do I make you nervous?" he asked in a low voice.

"No, you don't make me nervous. You are just always in the wrong place," she said. She took a step away from him and got a good look at what he was wearing for the evening. She had only seen him in white chef clothes, but now she knew this man looked good in everything. He had on a black suit that fitted him to a tee. In this suit, everyone could see he had broad shoulders that tapered down to a trim waist.

"You didn't even wait for me so I could pick you up," Evan said.

"You didn't return any of my calls or my emails so I couldn't confirm you were coming so I got myself here," she countered as he took her free hand and walked her toward one of the standing tables.

"I thought we were past this. I told you I'd be beside you throughout it all, and I thought you understood that I always keep my word," he said as he gazed into her eyes. "Did you really think I was going to leave you high and dry?"

"This was planned way before we met. You might have had plans," Pearla said.

"I wouldn't miss this for the world. I heard there's a 2-star Michelin chef serving here. I get to check out some of the competition and show off my new fiancée. It doesn't get better than that."

It wasn't until tonight that Evan had ever lost his date.

He didn't know what to do with her. He had read all of her emails, but his life had just been so busy trying to go to the shelter and teach classes that he hadn't had a chance to reply. He didn't think it was an issue. They had both agreed to this plan. Then why did she look so shocked to see him when they were at the party?

At first, he could tell she didn't know who he was. He waited for her to turn, then when she did, she dumped her soda on the front of his jacket. Now that they were past introductions, they were standing at the charity, and he could feel everybody's eyes on them. He took a sip of his soda and then leaned in close to whisper in her ear.

"Is the whole party going to be like this?"

"If you mean is everyone going to look at us for this event, then the answer is yes."

"So how long do we have to stay here while they look at us?"

"We don't have to stay long at all. I thank you very much for coming, and you can leave anytime you feel like it," she said through clenched teeth.

"I'm not going anywhere. Did I tell you how talented I think you are to be able to talk like that, barely moving your lips?"

She leaned away and glared at him.

"Now that's no way to be looking at your fiancé. I think you're supposed to have adoring eyes right now."

Before she could respond to him, a woman came by with two men in tow. She was on the short side, with blonde hair that was cut in a bob, and she was wearing a dress that had so many sparkles on it Evan thought it could land a plane.

"Hello, hello, hello, you two are the couple of the hour."

Evan smiled and nodded at her. Then she held out her hand for Evan to take.

"Forgive me interrupting your private conversation. I hadn't seen you before, and I always introduce myself to the newbies," she said to Evan. "I'm Nadia Mathews."

Evan nodded and took her hand. "I'm—"

"Oh, you don't have to tell me. I know who you are. You are Evan Carson, and you happen to be a Michelin chef. You are the proverbial son come back home. And if the headlines are to be believed, you and Miss Isaac's are engaged."

"I guess I feel special if you seem to know everything about me," Evan said, and both parties laughed.

"I don't know if you know, but it seems as though our Pearla has been a very popular woman this week."

"Really?" Evan said.

"First there was a rumor about her and Lance, and then you appeared."

"Lance, Lance, oh, yes, I do know Lance. Yes, he's a good friend and a great business associate to Pearla."

"Business associate, you say?" Nadia echoed. Evan watched her take sly glances at Pearla throughout the conversation. To her credit, she never gave a thing away.

"So you know Lance?" Nadia probed.

"Yes, we both know Lance."

Before Nadia could continue with her interrogation, Pearla cleared her throat.

"Nadia, I'm sure they'll be plenty of time to talk later. I see the two gentlemen behind you are patiently waiting. Would you like to conduct the business you came here for?"

Realizing this was the end of her conversation with Evan, she nodded graciously and gave him a smile before turning to Pearla.

"You are so right, Pearla. You know it's just so hard for me. I just don't get out enough with running all of these charitable events. Now, on to the purpose of the charity. As you know, we're here to ask for your support in young up-and-coming businesswomen."

"Of course," Pearla said as she pulled out a folded check. Nadia didn't open it. She just passed it to the gentlemen behind her.

"As always, thank you for your generous donation."

Nadia smiled at them both and then moved on to the next table. Evan waited until Nadia was two tables away.

"Can we leave now?"

"No, we can't," Pearla said with a small smile tilting the corner of her mouth. He reached out and placed his hand over hers on the table. He could feel her fingers trembling beneath his.

"Remember, we do this all the time," Evan whispered. Just then, Nadia looked over her shoulder and zeroed in on their touching hands.

Evan leaned in so he could whisper in her ear. "I want you to know I did wash my hands before coming here."

Her head popped up, and her laugh burst forth from her. "And you think that's the problem?"

He leaned his forehead against hers. "I was thinking that could be the only reason that you're trying to pull your hand away from me slowly."

Large brown eyes turned toward him. He could see a depth of emotion swirling there. "I don't know what to do."

He pushed his cola to the side. Then he brought his other hand up to trace her cheek and thread his hand into the edges of her hair. "The point is you don't do anything. This is when I sit here and just adore you."

Never in a million years would he have expected to see Pearla blush. She closed her eyes, and when she slowly opened them again, and the wariness was gone.

"Thank you."

"The pleasure is all mine, Pearla. I'm going to ask that famous question."

"What?"

"Can we leave now?"

Pearla pulled back and nodded. It seemed like she was avoiding his gaze.

"Of course. I'm sure everyone has seen enough." She pushed her soda away and pulled back her hand. Evan stopped her hand from moving, and she gave him a confused stare.

"I didn't want to leave because we were done. I just don't like sharing you in public."

"Why?"

"I just don't like sharing my treasures with anyone. I was hoping you'd let me take you out tomorrow?"

Pearla looked confused. "There are no events scheduled for tomorrow."

"The event will be you being out with me. Will you come out to play with me, Pearla?"

"Okay, Evan, I'll go out with you."

"Whew! I was worried there. I mean, just think what that would look like when a man can't get his fiancée to go on a date with him. That would be a new low for me."

"Enough, silly. How did you get here?"

"I brought my car, and you?"

"I took an Uber."

"I'll take you home, and tomorrow we'll go out, yes?"

"I said yes, already," she replied with a smile.

"Well then, my lady, come this way your carriage awaits."

Seventeen

It must have been the soda that made her agree to this. She was in several meetings today and on the phone for two long conference calls. During both of those occasions, while her body was there and she was responding to questions, her mind was lingering on the idea that tonight she had a date.

Several times she had thought about picking up the phone and coming up with some excuse on why she couldn't possibly make this date. It was the anticipation that was making it a hundred times worse than it needed to be. She could still hear the words that he said last night. He didn't want to share her.

She was able to figure out budgets, staffing issues, and even funding issues, but she wasn't able to come up with a way to get out of tonight's date. As the end of the day neared, she had to face it. She was beyond scared.

Finally, she got her nerve together, and she called him.

"Evan?" she said tremulously.

"I was expecting your call."

"Really?"

"Really. Before you speak, let me just say this, you're not calling to break your word now, are you? We're still going to go out, right?"

She snapped her jaw shut in frustration. She negotiated contracts for a living. She planned things that couldn't be planned. But right now, she was as trapped as a box turtle on its back. "Of course, I'm going out. I just wanted to confirm the time."

"Great! For a second, I thought you were calling to back out of our date."

"I don't back out of my commitments."

"Good. Wear something comfortable, and I'll see you at 5:30."

Comfortable? What was she supposed to put on that was comfortable? She was comfortable in her suits, but Pearla was pretty sure that Evan did not want her to wear one of those. She was going to ask him some more questions, to get some more details, when he hung up. She was left with a dial tone in her ear.

Pearla was still seething when she got home. When she walked into her apartment, she was not alone.

"You know it seems like you're here more and more these days," Pearla said.

"Your life has recently become way more interesting," Gloria replied with a smile.

Pearla had to make a decision. She either went into the bedroom and found some comfortable clothing or took the time to ask her sister to leave. She decided she'd spend time finding whatever "comfortable clothing" was.

"If you're going to be here, you should at least be helpful," Pearla said.

Gloria jumped off the sofa, clapping her hands. "Oh, goodie, I'm going to be the one to get the dirt first."

Pearla rolled her eyes. "You've made your point that I live a very boring life," Pearl muttered.

"Not boring, just predictable. I think Evan is the best thing for you."

"And you know this because…?"

"Because I've seen him. He really likes you. Not you the Project Manager or you the Business Owner, he really likes you Pearla," Gloria's eyes danced with excitement.

"He's my friend. And he's doing me a favor," Pearl said out loud. Maybe if she said it enough, she would believe it.

"Say what you want. But the truth is looking you in the face, and nothing you say will change that."

"Why does he like me now? Does he think I've changed?"

"I wasn't there when you two broke up the first time. What I can say is, I think he's always liked you. I just think now that we're all grown up, and you don't have all the responsibility of taking care of everyone anymore, now you have the ability to see that he really likes in you too."

What could she even say to that? There was so much truth in those words. How many times while Gloria was growing up had Pearla worked so much that sometimes she didn't even remember to eat much less have a love interest?

"Hey, Big Sis, don't mess this up."

Pearla nodded.

"Woohoo! I'm glad that tense moment is over. Now let's go find you some clothing," Gloria said.

"I can dress myself," Pearla protested.

"Some other night, but tonight we want to make sure we get the guy."

Evan was at Pearla's front door. Today was the kind of day that he had thought about canceling the date. However, one thing he'd learned was sitting at home and wallowing over something you couldn't change didn't make it any better.

He had woken up this morning with high hopes knowing he was going to see Pearla. Then Nancy called. One of the girls from the rescue, Twila was gone. Twila had packed up her bags, and her bed bunk was empty.

Evan should have known better. He should not have been surprised. Evan had been working in the shelters long enough to know that sometimes the women didn't stay. He had held out such great hope for Twila. When she had reached out to Pearla, he thought for sure Twila would be one of the ones who made it.

Trying to shake off the loss, he taught two more classes. Then the bitter blow came in the evening. Nancy called to let him know they had found Twila. She was in the hospital. Her condition wasn't clear, but Nancy would keep him informed.

When Pearla called, Evan thought it was just going to be the coup de grace on his day. The way he was feeling, he almost wanted her to cancel it. For a moment, he thought it would be better for him to cancel it so he could be at home with his disappointment.

He straightened up and knocked on the door. Evan tried to put on his best smile so that his melancholy mood didn't affect her. Then Pearla opened the door, and whatever he was feeling was whisked away. She wore a long dress. If his memory served him right, the women at the shelter told him this would have been called a maxi dress. The dress was a pale blue, and it had short sleeves and ruffles at the bottom. When she took a step back, he could see there were slits on the side of the dress that went to her knee. As she moved, he caught quick glimpses of her calf and blue and white sandals that wrapped around her ankle.

He must have been staring for a longer time than he knew.

"I knew this dress wasn't the right one. I can go change."

It was her determination to change the dress that brought him out of his trance. He looked up into Pearla's eyes and instead of seeing the confident woman he was used to seeing he saw a woman who was hesitant and waiting for him to say the right words.

"Don't change. You look perfect." With that being said, he held out his hand and waited for her to take it. Hand in hand, they walked to the car.

"Is your sister here?" he asked.

"No, you missed her. To be honest, she helped me get dressed for tonight. What's so weird though, is tonight she was extra happy."

"Really?"

"She had that secret smile on. Like she knew something that I didn't. She didn't want to talk about it either. Then after she had taken so much time to help me get dressed she said she had to run."

"It's hard to tell with kids that age," Evan said.

"Kids that age? ugh. Don't say that it only reminds me that I'm not in my twenties anymore."

"Then forget my slip of the tongue. Tonight you definitely don't look old, so let's put that thought from your mind."

After they were both seated in the car, she turned to him and asked the million-dollar question.

"Where are we going?"

"I can't tell you yet."

"What?"

"Just be patient and trust me."

He saw her sit back in her seat and could tell she was not a happy person. When he thought about where he was taking her, he wasn't sure she was going to be any happier either. The problem with good intentions, he thought. It was too late now though, everything was already set in place, he just hoped he hadn't made a huge mistake. The way the day was going, Evan wouldn't be surprised if this went wrong as well.

"You're really quiet. Are you okay?" Pearla asked.

He kept his eyes on the road and nodded. "Thanks for asking."

"Since I don't know where we're going. That means I don't know how much longer we have until we get there. Do you want to tell me about your day?" Pearla prodded.

Evan thought about Twila. He didn't want to depress Pearla. He thought instead about telling her something about the classes he taught today, and then he stopped himself. This was what he was asking for from her. If he wanted to get her confidence, he had to be willing to give his. More importantly, he had to trust her with his good days and his bad days.

"Twila left the shelter, and she's in the hospital."

"Oh, no, not Twila. I'm so sorry, Evan. Is she okay? I mean, obviously she's not okay if she's in the hospital, but you know what I mean."

She reached out and placed her hand on top of his on the steering wheel. "I didn't know that you had such a trying day. If I had known back at my place, we could have stayed in. We'll always have time to go out."

She never ceased to amaze him. Now more than ever, he was so glad he hadn't canceled, and that she hadn't either. "No Pearla, this is where I need to be. Sharing this moment about Twila with you is just what I needed to do to feel better. It's the sharing that makes all the difference."

"I'm here for you to share whatever your day holds."

"Thank you."

"For?"

"For being you."

He finally saw the turnoff in the road, and he slowed the car to take the exit.

"Why are we getting off here?" Pearla asked.

Evan didn't answer. He could tell Pearla was not happy about being surprised. She took her hand back and turned toward her window. The more they went down the road, the less happy she seemed to be. Then just before they had pulled up to the restaurant, Evan knew she saw all of the reporters there.

"Evan? Why is the press here? Why are we here?" she asked in a low voice.

"We're here for your party."

The sign hanging on the front door read, Congratulations to the Dynamic Duo.

She let out a breath, and he saw her clasp her hands in her lap.

"The press will be here all night?"

"No, they're only allowed outside the restaurant. We rented the whole restaurant, and inside, Gloria's calling it your Happy No Lance Day celebration."

She grinned. "She would. You said everyone?"

"Gloria, Catarina, Max, and Gloria invited some people from your company."

He waited for a reaction. Right now, she was so still, he wasn't sure how she was feeling.

"Gloria had the plan. I made the food, and Catarina rallied the people and the press together. My final contribution was to make sure you got here on time.

He parked the car and turned off the lights. He turned to her in the car and lightly touched her hand. When she turned toward him, he saw a panicked Pearla.

"I don't know if I can get out of the car Evan. Seeing all of these reporters and having to face all of the people inside makes me feel nervous. The people inside are the true challenge, they're not stock holders where their opinion doesn't matter," she said in a small voice.

He rubbed her hands to try to soothe her. "We're going to dance and have fun inside. We'll take care of the press first. Your friends are inside to help you relax."

"I'm not relaxed around a lot of people because I feel like I need to do things for them, to please them. And if I don't, I'll lose them. Lose them like I lost the men in my relationships—like I lost you."

Evan reached out and lifted Pearla's chin. He knew he needed to set things straight and comfort her. He waited for the words to come.

"Pearla, we're not here because you paid us to be, "he said in a low voice. "We're here because we are all blessed to be in your life. We're here because you give selflessly and never ask us for a thing, and we wanted to show you we're here for you. This party is a celebration of the woman you are and what you've done."

She looked over her shoulder. When their gazes met, he could see tendrils of doubt. Then the strength that had helped her build a company and take care of her family came back, and she put her shoulders back and then gave him a small smile.

"Well then, let's go. It would be rude to be late for my own party."

Eighteen

She had to trust Evan on this because right, now she felt like staying for the mandated amount of time and then slipping out the back. Still, Pearla forced herself to walk through the reporters with a smile on her face. She looked into the flashing cameras and heard the reporters call out that they looked like such a great couple.

"Do you have any comment about what Lance Gorman said?" a rather pushy reporter asked.

Pearla held her smile in place and let out a breath before she replied. "I'm sure that the comments from Lance must have been misinterpreted. He is a good associate that I work closely with."

"And the rumors about your engagement to him?" the reporter continued.

Evan stepped in. "There is an engagement. The reporter just got the wrong man. Now if you will excuse us, our friends and family are waiting."

"Can we come in?"

Evan put his hand at her back and guided her to the door. "No, this is a private affair."

The tingles that went through her as he moved them toward the restaurant door was just what she needed to pull herself out of the pit of despair she was slipping into.

After she got into the building, it was actually better than she expected. The decor was done to emulate a moonlit evening. There were lights and balloons everywhere, which was a definite sign that Gloria had been here. The lights and balloons were different shades of white, silver, and grey, making the ceiling sparkle as if they were outside.

The restaurant was called The Cove. Pearla hadn't been to this restaurant in a while. She had forgotten how pretty and spacious it was. The restaurant was a house that had been renovated and converted into a restaurant. When she looked around, she could see the hints of the home that used to be there. On all of the windows were plant boxes indoors, and on the walls were plaques of sayings like Bless this Mess.

As she and Evan walked into the restaurant, what surprised her the most was that there was a buffet. She looked over her shoulder at Evan. He shrugged.

"I couldn't be in two places at one time. Since I'm going to be sitting with the most beautiful woman in the place, I couldn't be serving the food as well. So, I had to make a decision. It was pretty easy to make."

Pearla knew Catarina would be there and Gloria. What surprised her was how many people from the company were there. Pearla had friends, but to see them come out here to see her was unexpected.

Natalie and Jackson Banner were here. Natalie was a believer who put her heart and soul into whatever she did. As soon as Natalie put her mind to something, you knew she was going to get it done. More than once, Pearla had depended on her to finish a project.

Gina Griggs—if it was in healthcare, she knew everything about it. She was a no-nonsense kind of woman. Pearla depended on Gina to be able to assess exactly what a situation was. There wasn't going to be a lot of fluff, but there was going to be truth and action items.

Even Cora was here. Cora was going to finally get her family. Cora and Michael were going from foster parents to adoptive parents. For as long as she could remember, Cora was always volunteering to help children. Finally, she was going to have children of her own. That she came out during this time to her party meant everything to Pearla.

Gloria sidled up next to her. "You know everyone is so happy you dumped Lance," Gloria said. She looked at her sister, who was looking very smug right now, and she looked around the room.

"Well, I can't tell you I really dumped Lance, now can I?"

"No, but what matters is that you were going to."

"So this party is about my intentions?"

"This party is about how you saved yourself from marrying a robot and how you switched your fiancé from a zero to a hero."

Pearla looked across the room to see Evan, who was smiling and dancing with Catarina. Evan was a catch no matter how she looked at it. Everyone loved him. He worked at a shelter. Gloria was right. Evan was the hero. Evan was everything a woman could ever want. The only problem now about the party was that she was the only one who knew the engagement wasn't real.

Pearla started to think about how upset Gloria would be if she slipped out the back door. More importantly, as she looked at Catarina, she felt guilty. Catarina had always been good to her and the fact that Catarina believed she was going to marry Evan, and she wasn't, started to weigh on her. Just when she was thinking about how to escape, she found herself looking into Nancy's eyes.

"Girl, you look like you're about to run out the door."

"That's not that far from the truth."

"It can be scary when you're falling in love."

"Is that what this is called?"

Nancy reached out and placed her hand on Pearla's shoulder. "He's a good man, do right by him."

What Pearla needed was some space. She smiled and waved at people as she went toward the restroom. When she got into the small corridor, she walked right past the restroom out into a small garden. It had a cherubim fountain in the middle of it, and on the circumference, there were several tall bushes. Some of the bushes were flowering, and some of them were evergreens. Right now, all of them looked peaceful to Pearla. The sound of trickling water and the lack of people gave her some time to think, or so she thought.

"Hello?"

Pearla almost jumped when she heard the voice. A blonde, slim woman appeared with a smile on his face.

"I'm sorry, I didn't mean to disturb you. I was already out here, but it's so hard to see anything with all the foliage and the fountain. I wanted to meet you."

Pearla looked at the woman but couldn't recall who she was. She tried to think of all the people she had been introduced to, but she couldn't place her. "I'm so sorry, I don't know, or don't remember your name," Pearla said hesitantly.

"We actually haven't met, so you didn't miss anything. Evan is the godfather to my little girl, Misty. I was on the planning committee for the party. I hope you like it."

Evan had let his family help with this party.

"I want to thank you so much for setting up everything."

"It was no problem. We would do anything for Evan. Especially when we see how happy he is, it's all worth it."

Pearla began to shift from foot to foot. "Listen—I'm sorry, your name?"

The woman smiled and shook her head. "How forgetful of me. To come all this way to want to say thank you to you and forgot to tell you my name. My name is Stacy."

"Look, Stacy, I don't want you to take this the wrong way, but Evan and I aren't really—"

"Oh, you're going to tell me about the fake engagement. Yes, Evan told us all about it."

"Then, I'm confused."

Stacy laughed. "I know that's how it started out, but I know Evan. This engagement is a lot of things to him, but fake isn't one of them. I just wanted to see the woman who has brought so much happiness to Evan. Enjoy the rest of the party."

Stacy left, and Pearla pressed her hand to her chest. It was time for the pep talk. She could do this. Pearla had earned this. Evan was so worth the risk. She was going to tell Evan the truth. Once she told him she loved him and that she was willing to take the big plunge, everything would get easier. It sounded really good right now. Pearla just needed to say it seven more times. She looked around the backyard and found a secluded flowering evergreen. Next to it was a small bench. It was perfect for her to sit and regroup.

After several calming breaths, she felt centered. She was going to walk out of this garden to find Evan tell him.

As she was leaving, she heard voices. No problem, she would just walk out the side and whoever was there would never know she had ever been there. She stood up and realized she recognized the people in the garden.

It was Catarina. She couldn't see the man's face because he had Catarina in his arms. It wasn't until she heard Catarina say, "Oh, Max." That Pearla gasped in shock at the site before her. "Max!"

Nineteen

It was as if her voice was a boom in the garden. Both of them jumped away from each other, and Catarina turned to Sea Pearl.

"Pearla, oh my goodness, I didn't see you."

"Yeah, I kind of got that," she muttered. Pearla was caught. Catarina had to be her mother's age, and to see her with Max was such a shock. What was she supposed to do, walk out or wait till they left?

"I can explain," Catarina responded.

"I think I'd like to hear this explanation," Evan said.

Catarina looked at Evan, and suddenly, she covered her face and began to cry. Max pulled Catarina into his arms and then gave Evan a stern look.

"She has done nothing wrong. You should be happy that you find her with a man who loves her. What you see here is my fault if there is any fault to be placed at all," Max said as he rubbed Catarina's back.

Pearla was caught between both parties. Any moment she thought she would be able to slip out, but then Evan came up behind her, blocking her escape.

"Evan, please don't think less of me," Catarina mumbled.

"Is that what you think? Is this what the argument has been about?" Evan asked.

"The argument has been about Max being so stubborn."

"There is no argument. Catarina wanted to pay me because I was helping her at the house. What man wants a woman to pay him when he intends to marry her?" Max said.

Catarina pushed away from Max and then faced him with her hands on her hips. "What man tells a woman that she must make a decision now? What kind of proposal is it to say I have to marry you or you will leave?"

"A man who has been waiting for you for a very long time. I'm getting old Catarina. Let's not waste any more time. I want to wake up next to you. Not wake up listening to you move around downstairs."

"That really seems reasonable Catarina," Evan interjected.

"Don't take his side!" Catarina responded. Then she looked at Pearla. "What do you think?"

Pearla looked at everyone watching her. She then looked over her shoulder at Evan. She knew this was the time. She looked at Catarina with all the compassion she felt in her heart.

"I think that love is the most important thing. When it comes, you should stop and accept it because you don't know how long it will last. Don't let your self-doubt get in the way. It's a precious gift."

Catarina looked at everyone and then turned to Max.

"You old goat. I love you. But I am set in my ways,

Max. What happens if you love me now only because you live where you do?"

"Is that your concern? Do you think there is anything you could do that would make me love you less? All of these years, we have been together. I've seen it all Catarina, and I'm still here."

Catarina turned to Evan.

"You won't mind, will you?"

"I think you are a grown woman and I'm a big boy. I don't mind giving up my room to get Max's apartment."

Catarina went to Evan, and he met her halfway and held her in his arms.

"Evan, thank you. Thank you for coming when I was being foolish and staying while I found my way."

Pearla looked at them and had to sniff the tears away. This was Evan, the man, who she saw being hugged by Catarina. The man who was encouraging a couple to love loudly. Pearla saw Max smile at Evan then give him a nod and leave. Pearla was scared and grateful for Max leaving and giving her and Evan the privacy they needed to sort things out. When Catarina pulled away from Evan, she wiped her cheeks and then motioned them both to sit with her on a nearby bench.

When they were all seated on the bench, Evan held Catarina's hand and placed a kiss on them.

Catarina looked at both of them.

"I understand what was wrong with Max and me. I don't understand what's wrong with the both of you?"

"Wrong?" Evan asked.

Catarina turned her focus to Pearla. "Was tonight a mistake? Was this party too much for you? Evan wasn't sure if this was going to be a good fit for you. But we wanted to make sure that your company was okay and that you two were okay."

Again, Pearla was taken back but how much Evan knew about her and how considerate he was. She could only hope as time went on that she would be that intuitive of him.

"Please don't worry about me. It was true it was unexpected, and normally I just don't like surprises. But tonight turned out to be better than I thought. I saw people from the company that I never expected to come out. And I met a very nice lady named Stacy who had only good things to say about Evan."

Catarina nodded her head. "When we came up with the idea, everybody wanted to come and help. Stacy offered to book the restaurant. Gloria said she would take care of the designs. We thought it was a good place for you to get rid of the old and start something new."

"Thank you."

"I think it's time for us all to clear the air about everything. If nothing else, what I have learned tonight is that we should always speak our hearts. I do not think you really know what happened when you left, Pearla."

Evan interrupted. "Catarina, there is no need to go into that. The past is the past."

"I disagree," Catarina protested.

"What is it? What is everybody talking about?" Pearla asked, looking between the two of them.

Catarina pushed Evan's hands aside and then held her hand out to Pearla. "Let me tell you a story about things that you do not know. When you and Evan broke up, he was distraught. He knew he was wrong, and there was nothing he could do about it. You are the reason that he works with the shelters. He wanted to give back, to go ahead and learn how to be responsible for someone besides himself. I have known for many years that his heart is yours. But it seems that the stubborn trait runs in us all. Sometimes only time can teach you something. Just make sure you two don't wait until you're as old as Max and me."

Catarina turned to Evan.

"Kids. I just don't understand you sometimes Evan. You speak all the time, but you don't speak when you need to. Have you told her your feelings? Have you told her that you came home looking for your heart before this engagement thing happened? There is a time to be stubborn, but if you are too stubborn, it becomes foolish and prideful."

Catarina stood and brushed off her skirt.

"Now, I have a man to go and educate on the proper way to propose to a woman. You two need to figure out what you are doing. You need to look past your fears and trust your feelings. I have done all I can do for now, and hopefully, you two will make the right decisions. If not, Gloria and I will be outside to help," Catarina said with a smile as she exited the garden.

Twenty

It was time.

He looked at Pearla and decided it was now or never. Strands of music drifted into the garden. He stood up and offered his hand.

"Would you like to dance?"

She put her hands in his tremulously. "I don't really know how to dance. I just kind of sway to and fro."

"It's okay. I've got two left feet, so I don't go far."

She settled into his arms, and they moved in silence to the music. Everything about her called to him. The scent of her wrapped itself around him and soothed an inner restlessness that he didn't know he had. The weight of her head against his shoulder made him feel ten feet tall. Catarina was right; this is who he had come home for. When the music stopped, they kept dancing. Then there was a loud applause inside from the party goers, and they stopped to look at one another.

"I know I've said it before, but thanks for the party."

"We have some unfinished business, do you want to run away with me, back to your place?" he asked.

She quickly looked over her shoulder and then back at him.

"Yes!"

"Let's go."

Evan walked to the back of the garden where there was a fence that opened to the garage.

"How did you know?"

"It was an old hangout before they decided to make it respectable."

"And what went on here before?" she teased.

"Lots of cooking with a 90-year-old grandma who didn't believe in writing recipes," he said. When he saw the coast was clear, he took her to the car. She was about to get in when he saw her smile.

"It's been fun, Evan."

He leaned down and placed a kiss on her lips. "It's not over yet."

They rode in silence, her head resting against the headrest. In no time at all, they were back at her condo.

When they got back to the condo, he stood at the door.

"If you're okay, I can leave now."

"Can you stay?"

"For—?"

"I want to cook."

Evan looked at her and nodded. When she went into her bedroom, he was nervous. She wanted to cook with him. He took off his coat and laid it on the couch. His hands were shaking. Pull it together, he said to himself. He could do this.

Evan went over every recipe he knew and tried to think of what she would pick.

"Umm. Evan?"

He almost jumped when he heard her.

"Yes, yes, I'm coming. What are we making?" He couldn't say anything beyond that after he saw her. Pearla's hair was down, and she was dressed in a soft pink top and grey sweats. It reminded him of what she wore in college.

"Flan. It's a comfort food for me," she said with a smile.

"I'll let you lead."

Her smile grew wider. "Thank you. Why don't we start with the caramel, that will be the top anyway? I'll get the pans."

He knew how to make flan. He put the saucepan on the stove. Then he got the sugar, put it into the pan, and then put water in the pan.

"You're putting water in the sugar?" she asked.

"Yes, you can make a hard crystalized caramel, or you can take your time. Let me show you."

When the sugar turned into a syrup, he covered it. She looked over his shoulder with doubt in her eyes.

Evan laughed. "The water from the top will fall into the sugar mix and keep it from getting hard in the pot." A few minutes later, she wanted to stir it. Instead, he showed her how to swirl the pot so the sugar syrup would stay consistent. When it was a dark amber, she poured it into the pan.

"I'm tired," Evan joked. "It's hard teaching."

Pearla laughed and scooted him to the side. "Teaching, huh? I've got the custard."

"Okay, I'll be quiet because you know, no matter what you make, I'll still care about you."

"Whatever," she said, laughing at him. She poured the milk, sugar, and eggs into the pot. When she was finished with the custard, he set the flan up, and they both congratulated one another on their work.

"I've been stalling long enough," she said. "I think we're both ready."

"You don't want to wait until we see how the flan comes out?"

Pearla laughed. "No, you're fate isn't resting on the flan, just my bragging rights. I want you to know that I love you, Evan. I didn't want to be vulnerable, and I was afraid."

"I was afraid too, Pearla. It's hard to think no matter what you do, you won't measure up, and I didn't think I did."

He leaned over and placed his lips on hers. Pearla's lips were soft and sweet like a dessert he could never get enough of. He lingered for a moment and then pulled back. He reached for her hands and kissed each finger.

"I love you, Pearla."

Pearla let out a big sigh. "Whew! I'm glad you said it, because I was getting a little worried there."

He reached out and tucked a lock of hair behind her ear. "You never have to worry. I'm yours."

Epilogue

In the air wafted the smell of flan and caramel pumpkin bread. Both of the scents were dark and rich signifying the end of summer and the beginning of fall. It was a time of preparation for new beginnings. Pearla couldn't think of a better time to have her wedding. Catarina had allowed them to use the school to have their wedding.

Pearla was putting dollops of homemade cream on top of slices of caramel pumpkin bread. Evan had cut the bread and plated each of the 45 plates and she as putting the final touch on them.

Gloria came by and shook her head as she watched Pearla.

"Who serves at their own wedding?"

Pearla smiled. "We do."

Gloria shrugged her shoulders and then looked over at Evan who was also preparing at another table.

"You two didn't even do the first dance."

"We can always dance. We both thought it was important that the first dance was Max and Catarina. Don't despair Gloria we at the first slices of bread and cake," Pearla said wistfully.

Throwing her hands up in the air Gloria stood with her arms crossed over her chest. You two are made for each other. I'm glad you found each other because this thing you two are doing is just weird. As long as you're happy."

"I am," Pearla reassured Gloria.

"I'll be back, I'm off to get you some seltzer water. Watching you is making me sweat."

Pearla watched Gloria go and saw Twila sitting in a chair talking to Nancy. Pearla thought back to the day Twila had been released from the hospital. She had tried to go home and pick up her items but was caught by her boyfriend at the last moment, hence the hospital care.

When Pearla looked at her now, no one would be able to tell that she had just gotten released in the last week. After she gotten out of the hospital she had nowhere to go. Pearla and Evan found her an apartment and Catarina gave her help job at the school. Now Twila looked confident and strong.

Catarina and Max continued to dance on the floor. It was as if they didn't every want to leave each other's arms. Pearla looked to them and hoped she was looking at a view of her future with Evan. Catarina was looking into Max's eyes as if he were the only man in the room. She had pink and white floral dress. The sleeves were off the shoulder and the dress stopped mid-calf. Max looked just as dashing in his dark blue suit. He had eyes for Catarina only as well.

Her wedding had been exactly what she wanted. The ceremony had been held in the school. The bride and groom catered the event and they got the students to serve. Evan had dressed in a dark chef's outfit and Pearla had dressed in a white one. Pearla knew her father would have loved this ceremony.

Evan was her husband. It was still surreal to her. Evan was her husband and they were working side by side. She couldn't help but stop ever so often and look at him at the cake table slicing the remainder of their cake and plating it for others to come by and pick it up at their leisure.

Sure enough he looked up as if he could feel her looking at him. As if on cue the both of them smiled at one another and she quickly looked away.

"For real! You two are married. It's over. Stop mooning at one another," Gloria teased.

Pearla took the drink Gloria offered and looked over at Evan. He was helping some guests serving cake. You could see he was so happy that it made her heart fill to the brim with how much she respected and loved him.

Pearla thought about life before Evan. She couldn't believe that she as on the verge of giving up on having a true love in her life. Then Evan had come back and they both of them had reaffirmed their faith in life and love again. They didn't agree on everything but they most times they settled it in a cook off and a visit from Gloria to get the spoils.

Stacy came over to her table and gave her a once over. "This is not the way I imagined you on your wedding day. Why don't you let Gloria finish that up?"

Gloria chimed in. "You I absolutely would finish that bowl of whip cream up."

Pearla laughed. "Gloria she means put it on the bread slices."

Gloria gave Stacy a frown. "Tell her you didn't mean that Stacy."

Pearla laughed at them both before stopping them.

"Guys, there's no need to argue. I wouldn't leave this table until I'm finished no matter what."

Stacy peered over at Evan who was also working away. "Is this some kind of chef thing? If that's what works for you both."

Gloria looped her arm into Stacy's. "Let's go before the work becomes contagious."

Pearla thought of Stacy as a sister. They were both about the same age and they were developing a special relationship with Gloria as well. The music slowed down and one of her favorite love songs began. Max tapped her on her shoulder and held out his hand. "While I'm proud to show off my love to everyone. It's time for the bride to take the floor."

She thought about saying now until she saw Catarina had tapped Evan on the shoulder as well. She went with him and when she saw Catarina with her hand in Evans' she expected them all to dance. Instead, Catarina and Max presented them to each other.

Pearla looked at Max. "Certainly you did not expect me to dance with you before your husband."

Max and Catarina left them on the dance floor and Evan held out his hands. Pearla went into his embrace and rested her head on his shoulder. They were surrounded by friends and family. Pearla couldn't have planned this any better if she tried.

"So Mrs. Carson, is it all you thought it was going to be?" he asked, as she felt his breath tickle her ear lobe.

She looked up at him and smiled. "I didn't know it until I saw it but yes this is everything I want and more."

He pulled her closer and sighed in her hair. "You are my dream made manifest. I love you Pearla."

"I love you more Evan."

I hope you enjoyed Pearla and Evan's story. I've enjoyed the women of Vision Consulting and the men who love them. If you've enjoyed reading this book, please take a moment to write a review.

Sign up to my newsletter to receive updates on new releases, sale promotions, and free books.

susanwarnerauthor.com